PAST TENSE

PAST TENSE

Star Spider

HarperCollins*Publishers*Ltd

Published by HarperCollins Publishers Ltd

First edition

HarperCollins books may be purchased for educational, business,
or sales promotional use through our Special Markets Department.

HarperCollins Publishers Ltd
2 Bloor Street East, 20th Floor
Toronto, Ontario, Canada
M4W 1A8

www.harpercollins.ca

Library and Archives Canada Cataloguing in Publication
information is available upon request.

ISBN 978-1-44345-211-3

Printed and bound in the United States
LSC/H 9 8 7 6 5 4 3 2 1

For Ben—you are my hero.

1.

My mom and I were born on the same day. Every year on our birthday she would kiss me and hug me and tell me, "You're the best birthday present I could have asked for, Julie." I never said it back, but I should have.

Lorelei tells me my breath smells like pork rinds so I hit her in the arm. Then she screeches and says, "You're the worst friend ever, Julie," and my heart hurts a little because I can't stand the idea that Lorelei thinks I'm the worst friend ever. And then Mr. Gomez comes over and pulls me away to give me a stern "talking to." Totally condescending, of course, because I don't think Mr. Gomez has really clued in to the fact that we are in grade nine and completely capable of handling our own issues.

"Violence isn't the answer to the problems of the world," Mr. Gomez says, his voice dropping low to keep our conversation private.

I know that, obviously. "Of course," I reply. It's not that I wanted to hurt Lorelei or anything; it's just that I wanted to tell her in a physical way that I was wounded by the pork rind comment. I guess the hit was also an excuse to touch her.

"It's best to use our words to resolve conflict," he continues.

I smile at him to show I'm listening.

I think Mr. Gomez might be in love with me, because he often gives me stern "talkings to" in my history and world issues classes—he's my teacher in both. But when he pulls me aside he always has this little smile on his lips like my dad has when I'm getting in trouble. It's a smile that says he's not pleased but still completely charmed. Plus, Mr. Gomez pronounces my name "Jewel-ie," instead of just plain old "Julie" like everyone else. I think he's probably trying to emphasize that he thinks I'm jewel-like, which is nice and flattering, I guess. The truth is I feel a little bad for Mr. Gomez. He often stays late at school, and sometimes when I'm walking home I turn around and see him gazing longingly out the window at the clouds or wherever. So because I feel bad for him, and because I suspect he might be in love with me, I nod very sincerely while he talks. I try to look him directly in the eyes too, because Mom says eyes are the windows to the soul. Mr. Gomez possibly lacks a bit of soul in his life, but I have plenty to spare; maybe I can transfer some to him via eye contact.

I'm not interested in Mr. Gomez sexually, of course, because all of my romantic feelings are reserved for Lorelei. But looking in his eyes isn't so bad: they are brown with a little rim of gold around the irises. I imagine he likes that aspect of himself, although I hope he appreciates other things about his face too; like his strong nose that looks like a beak on some sort of majestic bird—an eagle, maybe. I heard somewhere that some people believe certain high-flying eagles have touched the face of God. This always struck me as ludicrous. Only little kids think God lives *in* the clouds. Adults understand that God is more a lofty state of mind than a real person with a real face living somewhere. But I only know this because I'm fully an adult now, having recently turned fifteen, which everyone knows (and Lorelei says) is the gateway age to true mental maturity.

After a few more of Mr. Gomez's catchphrases about problem-solving through diplomacy, I'm finally released. I notice that Lorelei doesn't look angry anymore; in fact, I'm not sure she was really angry to begin with. So I approach her and smile my most sincere and authentic smile. Then she holds out her hand and we go off to the washroom, hands clasped like two ends of a necklace, our best-friendship fully restored.

In the hall on the way to the washroom, we pass Henry Carter. Lorelei dated Henry for about two months but then broke it off, claiming she wanted someone more mature. I wasn't sad to see Henry go. Although he's technically the best-looking boy in our grade, he's also a little vapid. Lorelei and I discussed his lack of soul many times before she eventually severed their connection. I suppose my intentions in those discussions weren't always honourable, but he moved on so quickly to dating Gabriela Souza that I don't feel bad for him at all.

Henry is striding down the hall in typical Henry fashion—shoulders squared, gaze straight ahead, an overconfident bounce in his step. He's always flouncing around the place like the cock of the walk, never noticing that there are totally other people in the world.

"Hi, Henry," Lorelei says, to catch his attention.

At the sound of his name Henry looks over. He glances at me first, and for a tiny fraction of a second it seems like he's going to smile. Then his gaze flits over to Lorelei and a sly, gross grin slathers itself across his face.

"Hey, Lorelei . . . lookin' good today," he says.

I roll my eyes and press myself against the lockers to try to escape the smell of his cologne. I hate that smell. Lorelei always used to be covered with it when she and Henry were dating. It was a depressing reminder of how often she ditched me for him or used me as an excuse to cover with her parents when they were out together.

Lorelei smiles at him, this big smile that suggests she's happy with his attention, but she doesn't reply to his compliment. She just pulls me away through the hall.

When we get into the washroom I'm relieved to be away from Henry. It's also empty, which is perfect because I love the way Lorelei's voice echoes off the brown-tiled walls and I wouldn't want anyone interfering with that.

"So, what did *he* say to you?" Lorelei asks conspiratorially once the door is closed. At first I think she's talking about Henry, but then I realize she actually means Mr. Gomez. She always refers to Mr. Gomez with a bit of reverence in her pronouns. Probably because it's more dramatic that way.

"He was totally being all high and mighty, as usual. He told me it wasn't right to hit people, and that I should say I'm sorry. So, I'm sorry," I say. "What's a pork rind, anyway? I've never smelled one."

She sighs in a movie star kind of way that she's picked up recently from the old black-and-white channel that she stays up late to watch with her mother and doesn't tell her father (who's a pastor) about. The "clandestine womanly bonding times," as she refers to them.

"Father brought them home last week and they're all right, I guess, in a greasy sort of way. They smell kind of meaty. I suppose I should say I'm sorry too . . . it's not your fault you have bad breath," she says.

It's not like she's trying to be mean—she's just being honest—but I must admit to being crushed by her declaration about the badness of my breath. I had hoped that at some point soon we could progress from hand-holding to practice kissing, as Josie Khan and Carla Reyes are rumoured to be doing in Carla's basement at their Friday night sleepovers. But no one wants to kiss someone with pork-rind breath. I tear myself away from the mirror and lean against the wall, attempting to look casual despite my distress.

"Father says pork rinds aren't good for us though, so we have to limit our intake," she continues, fishing around in her pocket and pulling out her Brave Red MAC lipstick. Lorelei is the kind of girl who calls her parents Mother and Father, which seems very old-fashioned to me. I went through a stage when I was thirteen of addressing my parents by their actual names, Olive and Maxwell, but Olive started crying and said it was too soon, so I went back to calling them Mom and Dad again.

"Well, too much of a good thing, I guess . . . ," I say. My words trail off because of the distraction of Lorelei's pouty lipstick application and my own inner struggle for and against telling her about my deep and unrelenting desire to stick her lips to mine.

In this day and age in Toronto it's all right to be queer. Everyone's pretty much okay with it. But Lorelei's family situation is complex because of the aforementioned pastorness of her father. So I'm obviously conflicted. They aren't Catholics or Westboro Baptists or anything, but they are Anglican. And there isn't a little rainbow flag on the door of the Anglican church like there is on the door of the Unitarian church a block away from my house. I figure if the Anglicans were really open to that sort of thing they would definitely advertise it: these days it's all about advertising your beliefs so people know where they belong. We're agnostic. Actually, Mom says she's atheist, but I think it's up for debate. Dad says it's illogical to be completely atheist because you just never know, and whenever he says that Mom nods, so I have to assume she's open-minded to the possibilities. In terms of my innermost thoughts though, I prefer to not be limited in my options. I took a class on world religions in grade eight, and I'm definitely inclined toward Buddhism. Plus, I have a very strong interest in Bahá'í, which I plan to research, beyond a simple Wikipedia investigation, when I get my act together.

Lorelei pops the cap back on her lipstick, presses her touched-up lips together, then smiles very, very wide. I wonder what she's thinking but, as usual, I don't ask. She flips her wavy blond hair dramatically and bunches it over one shoulder so it looks like a golden waterfall cascading over her body. She stands very straight and looks confidently into the mirror. This pose is the epitome of Lorelei: the reason I fell in love with her. It's the stance of a girl who knows exactly who she is and what she wants—an unshakable certainty.

"Do you want to sleep over Friday night?" she asks.

I perk up at this because I think that maybe *sleep over Friday night* is a code indicating that she's heard about Josie and Carla's kissing practice. So I lean even more intently against the wall in my effort to be casual and say, "Of course."

"Good. Mother will bake some cookies, and I just got a new game called Truth or Dare. It's essentially Truth or Dare but with playing cards, so we don't always have to think of everything ourselves," she says. Then she rolls her eyes in the mirror. "Obviously we're too old for Truth or Dare, but it can be our little secret, right?"

I smile at her and nod as she rinses her hands and runs them through her hair. And I hope beyond hope that one of the cards makes reference to kissing.

"Purrrfect," I say in a strange accent that sounded better in my head.

She giggles and holds out her hand. Then we head back to class, where we are learning about Ptolemaic Egypt in history and I can almost see Lorelei imagining herself as Cleopatra—complete with snake armbands and heavy charcoal eyeliner.

Thankfully, after school there are no more Henry Carter sightings. Lorelei and I walk home together and she wears her new sunglasses that she refers to as "cat-eyed." She bought them at a vintage store in Kensington Market. Lorelei loves Kensington Market; she says it's the beating heart of the city and everyone there is so much more chill than the people in our tame middle-class neighbourhood in the east end of Toronto. While I agree that Kensington Market is interesting, I do like how calm and clean our neighbourhood is in comparison.

"How do they look?" she asks, adjusting the glasses.

"Amazing," I say. I find it hard to imagine anything looking bad on Lorelei, mostly because she has a flawless complexion and her teeth are perfect and white. She got her braces off last summer, and on the first day of grade nine she was instantly surrounded by guys at lunch. She was already one of the prettiest girls in school, and that kind of transformation gives you even more of an edge. So she was, and still is, one of the hottest commodities on the market. I have to admit this makes me a little nervous. Sometimes, especially at perfect moments like this, I worry that she's just too cool for me. Like maybe there's someone she would rather be walking home with, someone she would rather be showing her cat-eye glasses off to. It's not outside the realm of possibility. She does, after all, have at least one million more friends than I do.

The sun is still shining as we make our way home. I peek back once and, because his classroom faces the street, I see Mr. Gomez in the window, looking out with a certain tension in his face. I don't discuss it with Lorelei though. I don't want the focus of our walk to be Mr. Gomez and his feelings for me—a little secret I have yet to share with her. I want the focus to be on Lorelei and *her* potential feelings for me.

"So, it's May," I say, super casually. "Do you have any plans for the Spring Fling?" The Spring Fling is our first official high-school formal. There have been some smaller dances throughout the year, and of course there were a few in grades seven and eight, but this is the real deal—the main event.

She sighs again and sashays a little. "There's a distinct lack of maturity amongst the student body, Julie. It's, like, such a disappointment. I'll probably just go stag, and we can be two single girls on the prowl."

She shoots me a questioning look. "Unless, of course, you have someone in mind?"

"No." I'm sure I say it entirely too quickly: it's practically overlapping her previous sentence. "No, you're right, we should just go together . . . alone."

She turns her cat eyes toward me. I can't see her real eyes, but she does raise her eyebrows in a suggestive sort of way that makes my stomach clench. Suggestive of what doesn't matter, because suggestive of anything with Lorelei makes me dizzy.

"Purrrfect," she says.

And I laugh.

Lorelei drops me off at my house. I watch her sashay away under the auspices of a concern for her safety. I really do feel bad not telling her about my feelings, but there's no way to approach the whole being-in-love-with-her situation other than slowly and carefully.

After she turns the corner and passes out of sight I unlock the door and go inside. Our house is a cavernous old thing that Mom says was built in the early 1900s, and I believe it. It's drafty and creaky and smells in some places of old brick and in many places of dust. Sound echoes in the kitchen, and there's a terrifying basement that I avoid, not because I'm really that scared, but mostly because it's super damp down there and recently, in health class, I learned about certain airborne bacteria that breed in damp conditions.

As soon as I open the door I notice something is

different. It's darker than usual, and the sound of my baby brother JC's screams are ripping through the house. JC is short for James Christopher, James being Mom's father, now deceased, and Christopher being Dad's father, who lives in Florida with a woman named Fran who Dad can't talk about without frowning.

I stand in the doorway for a moment, unsure what to do. There might be an intruder, or there might have been an accident, or Mom might have vanished, or any number of things I don't want to think about. My heartbeat picks up its pace and I can feel the pulse of it crawling around under my skin.

"Mom!" I yell. No answer. JC pauses a moment in his wailing and I listen very hard to hear if Mom has scooped him up and is reassuring him into silence. But soon he starts howling again.

"Mom!" I call, louder this time.

Again no answer. A brief pause from JC. Then another round of anguished baby screams. I hesitate only a second longer before I run upstairs to JC's rescue and lift him from his crib into my arms. Lifting before smelling was my first mistake. JC reeks like only babies can reek, which is an absolutely putrid and practically inhuman form of torture. But as bad as it is for me, I'm sure it's worse for him. In fact, I can see it etched into his scrunched-up little baby face. I think about calling for Mom again, but at this point JC is in my arms and it will hurt his tiny baby ears if I do. So instead I do the most reasonable thing: drop my backpack, hold my breath and change his diaper.

I insisted on learning to change JC's diaper when he arrived home six months ago because I wanted to be responsible. I didn't realize how disgusting it was though: How could I? All the lifelike baby-related toys for kids, like Little Suzy Pees-A-Lot, are bogus representations. They wouldn't be lifelike unless you added ammonia and yellow food dye to Little Suzy's plastic bladder. But no one ever does that because it would obviously turn all the would-be future mothers off kids forever.

Once JC is dry he smiles at me in a rather beatific way, and with his diaper safely disposed of in the smell-proof waste bin I suddenly remember what I love about him. I dance him around a bit and sing him snippets of the latest Katy Perry song as I undertake the adventure of searching the house for my wayward mom. I choose to see it as an adventure so I won't be completely comatose with fear, but the truth is I'm a bit shaky. I have to keep bouncing JC around—I feel like I might drop him at any moment if I hold still.

I'm not in the mood to call out for Mom anymore; in fact, I'm not interested in making any kind of noise at all. So, as I go from room to room on the second floor, I creep around like a burglar. And although I try not to let them in, right before I round every corner my brain fills up with these horrible images of Mom lying flat on her back covered in blood and guts. It's the scariest time I can remember having in ages, much scarier than that stupid haunted house they had a couple of Halloweens ago at Community Centre 45, which they advertised as the scariest half hour of your life, even though it was just a few teenagers in horse masks and a bowl full of peeled grapes. Plus, everyone kept checking their phones every five seconds, so the whole place was always illuminated and you could easily see the horse-headed teenagers hiding behind chairs and under tables.

Luckily we seem to be alone.

After searching the whole top floor, I head downstairs and continue my efforts, JC still in my arms. The parlour is clear. So are the living room and the dining room. Finally I make my way to the kitchen, where Mom is standing stock-still at the sink, arms submerged up to the elbow in murky grey dishwater. She's staring straight ahead, out the window above the sink, and it should look completely normal, but it doesn't. Something is wrong.

"Mom?" I say, taking a tentative step toward her.

She doesn't move, not even a blink or a flinch to indicate she heard me.

"Mom?" I say again, louder this time.

Nothing.

JC fidgets in my arms, looking toward Mom like he's ready to be handed over. But she's not moving. I take another step forward. Her eyes are so wide, but they look unfocused, like she's staring hard at something but not really seeing anything. My heart is a lump in my throat. What's wrong with her? Why isn't she moving? How long has she been standing here with her hands in that greasy water? I don't know what to do. I take another step and now I'm right beside her. I hear the soft push of her breath as it goes in and out. At least she's breathing. I shift JC so he's resting in the crook of one arm and reach my free hand toward Mom's shoulder.

She's wearing an old T-shirt that's soft and worn. It feels familiar, but she doesn't. Her shoulder is stiff and unmoving beneath my fingers.

"Are you okay?" I whisper. I'm on the verge of tears now but I have to keep it together. She's probably just lost in thought. Or something. "Mom?"

She doesn't turn when I touch her, or snap out of it or anything. But she does speak. It takes a moment, and it's so quiet I almost don't catch it, but they are definitely words and they are definitely weird.

"I can't feel my heartbeat."

JC squirms around like he's trying to break free, and I'm so startled I almost drop him.

"What do you mean?" I ask.

None of the tension has left the air, and Mom is still frozen and staring straight ahead, but at least she gave me something.

"My heart," she says, "it's gone."

Her lips barely move when she speaks, and her words barely make it to my ears, so I'm not sure I've heard them correctly.

"Your heart is gone?" I ask.

"Gone," she murmurs.

I shake my head. This is getting ridiculous. "No," I say. "It's not gone. It's right where it always is."

Then she looks at me. She turns her head slowly and looks straight into my eyes, and for a long, terrible second I think that maybe she's telling the truth. Her eyes don't look like normal Mom eyes. They look empty and hollow and filled with a sadness that I have never seen eyes filled with before. My stomach clenches hard and I have to turn away.

When I look back she's turned her head to the window again and I don't know what to do, so I use my free hand to pull her arms gently out of the dishwater. Her fingers are wrinkled and pasty white. I stick my own finger in the water; it's definitely room temperature, if not cold, so I imagine she's been standing here for hours, just staring out into the backyard thinking about her missing heart. I use a cloth to dry her hands, and a shadow of a smile appears on her face.

"Thanks," she says.

Is this my real mom? Maybe she just needed a little brain vacation. She's been more tired than usual lately, so maybe she just needed some time to zone out and think about the state of her heart. It makes sense—right? I guide her over to the kitchen counter and sit her down on the stool. JC is squirming even harder now, like he wants to jump out of my arms and into hers, so once she's seated, I fold her arms into a cradle shape and place him gently into them.

"There," I say, "that's better, right?"

"Better," she whispers.

Now that I've let go of JC, a bit of the nervousness and panic of the last few minutes washes out of me and I feel lighter. I don't have to be the responsible one anymore; that's Mom's job.

"Okay now?" I ask.

Mom is looking at JC like she's forgotten his name.

"Okay now," Mom says quietly. "Sorry."

I'm not convinced, but I don't want to stick around any longer, so I run upstairs to my room and shut the door tight behind me.

2.

When I was two my mom taught me the word *happy*. She told me about how she would say it over and over in different voices while she made funny faces, trying to entice me to repeat it. And she was so thrilled when I finally said it back: "happy." She wanted to teach me a word that would define my life, something that would stay with me.

At dinner the house is filled with the smell of macaroni and cheese. I haven't exactly been hiding in my room: I've been doing actual stuff like homework, which involves struggling to study for an upcoming math test despite being preoccupied with Mom's space-out and missing heart. I may have also been looking at my mostly flat chest in the mirror and wondering if Lorelei would prefer me without boobs. Kelly Mitchell's cousin Francis has two mothers: according to her, one is butch and one is femme. I heard that the femme has more in the boob department, so I was thinking that I could be the butch and Lorelei could be the femme.

When Mom calls me I head downstairs slowly. The truth is I don't want to see her and remember what happened earlier. I've been trying to put it out of my mind, write it off as just a weird moment, no big deal.

The dining-room table is set for dinner and the setting sun is shining through the windows, making everything a hazy orange. Dad is nowhere to be seen (as usual), and JC is in his basket in the corner sleeping. I take a seat and listen to the sound of Mom in the kitchen.

"Do you need any help?" I call.

"No, coming," Mom replies. Her voice still sounds soft and quiet, and I try not to let it bother me. She's probably just tired from being with JC all day and doing all the mom stuff she does. An image of her grey-dishwater-pruned hands flashes through my mind, but I push it away because it brings a shiver of panic with it. *I can't feel my heartbeat.* No. There's nothing to panic about. Mom's fine. It was nothing.

Mom comes in from the kitchen wearing her oven mitts and clutching a big glass pan of macaroni. Then she pauses and looks really hard at the macaroni, like she's just spotted a bug in it or something, and for a second it seems as if she's going to drop the hot pan onto the floor. I can't explain it because she doesn't actually do it, or even loosen her grip, as far as I can tell; it's just a feeling I get. I *feel* like she's going to drop the pan. Instead she takes one, two, three steps forward and thunks it down on the table. I smile at her but she barely glances at me.

"Thanks," I say.

"Yeah," she replies before disappearing back into the kitchen. JC shifts in his basket and I dole out a too-big portion of macaroni for myself. I've been starving since lunch.

I start eating before Mom returns with the salad. Usually she rolls her eyes when I do that, but this time she just slides into her chair. Then she dishes herself out a pile of salad and eats really slowly.

"When's Dad coming home?" I ask, trying to get the conversational ball rolling.

Mom looks up at me, finally, and smiles a bit. "As soon as he can." Her eyes don't seem as empty as they did in the kitchen earlier, but she still looks kind of out of it.

"He's been working so much lately," I reply.

"Things are a bit tight," she says. "I mean, we're fine, but he has to take more on while I stay with JC."

"Still, it sucks we never see him." Maybe that's what Mom's sad about. Maybe she and Dad just need a vacation or something. They've both been pretty stressed out lately, Mom with JC and Dad with work.

And I have noticed that they've been tense around each other too; they don't seem to talk as much as they used to. I don't know what's going on with that, but it's been that way for at least as long as JC's been around, if not longer.

"Yeah," Mom whispers. She takes a slow bite of salad. She's barely touched her food, but I'm already half-finished my first helping.

"Are you okay?" I ask. "I mean, earlier you were . . . "

Mom glances up at me and a look I don't recognize passes over her face. "I'm fine," she says quietly.

"I just think maybe you should talk to Dad, get him to give you some time off JC duty or something?"

She frowns at me, her shoulders hunched. "No. It's fine. Don't worry about it, honey. Let's just leave Dad out of this, okay? Keep it just between us? I don't want him to have any extra stress on his plate."

This doesn't seem like something I should be keeping to myself, but if Mom wants it to be a secret, I can keep it.

"Okay . . . ," I say.

JC lets out a little chirp and I turn to look at him, but it was nothing; he's still fast asleep.

Mom lifts up a piece of lettuce and nibbles the edge of it.

"Aren't you hungry?" I ask.

"I ate a big lunch," she murmurs.

But she doesn't look like she ate a big lunch. In fact, she looks thinner than I can ever remember her looking. She's a firefighter—at least she was before she had JC—so she usually has pretty big heroic-mom muscles. But since she gave it up, she's lost a bunch of weight, and now she looks like she can barely lift her fork.

But before I can say anything about her lunch, or lack thereof, I hear a key in the lock and Dad is rushing into the dining room. He says hi to me, drops his bag on the floor and walks over to Mom to kiss her hello. Their lips don't even touch. I try to remember the last time I actually saw them hug or really kiss, but I can't. How long *have* they been this distant?

"Sorry I'm late. I barely got out alive this time," Dad says. He chuckles at his own joke but it doesn't sound like a usual Dad laugh; it sounds wilted and exhausted. Both of my parents are such zombies right now. Dad grabs a huge serving of macaroni and starts wolfing it down before he's even sitting.

"So hungry," he says with his mouth full.

"How was work?" I ask.

Dad is a computer systems analyst. Mom always used to joke that she doesn't even know what that means, to which Dad would reply that *he* doesn't know what it means either.

"Good, good," Dad says, still completely focused on his food.

I've finished my first serving and now I'm onto my second. I haven't even touched the salad yet, and usually Mom would bug me to eat my greens, but not tonight, apparently.

"I hit Lorelei today at school," I say, partially because I'm feeling confessional and partially to see if Mom will react. Dad glances at Mom but she doesn't look up from her plate, so he puts his fork down for a second and looks at me.

"Why did you do that?" he asks.

"Because she said my breath smelled like pork rinds."

He laughs in one quick, short burst and I join in. Then he stops and tries to look disapproving instead. I try to stop laughing too.

"Well, that wasn't very nice of you, was it?" he says. But he's cracking that little charmed smile that he and Mr. Gomez share, so I know I'm in the clear.

"No, it's not . . . buuuut I said sorry and everything and she forgave me so we're cool." I elongate the word *but* because Dad has a history of thinking elongated words are cute.

"Olive?" Dad glances at Mom again, but still she doesn't look up.

"Olive?" he says again, louder this time.

Mom's eyes snap to his face, but her expression is still blank. "Listen to your father." Her voice sounds quiet and hollow, like it's coming from a distance. I try to ignore it.

Dad nods and smiles, then looks back at me and frowns. I grin at him, showing both rows of teeth, and he looks down at his plate to try to hide his smile. Dad's easy. Usually Mom is the tough one. They used to have the good cop/bad cop thing down pat, but now it's like the good cop is all on his own. He picks up his fork and goes back to mowing down his meal. I want to tell him about the weirdness with Mom today but I don't want to betray her confidence. So instead I just silently hope Dad notices how odd and quiet she's acting.

It's silent for a while except for Dad's chewing noises and mine, and the clink-clink of Mom's empty fork on her plate. Dad looks off over my head at nothing in particular and his eyelids start to droop a bit, like he's falling asleep mid-chew. Eventually, all the chewing and the clinking start to get to me.

"I'm sleeping over at Lorelei's on Friday," I announce. I try to make it sound like it's a done deal, not open for debate. Although with Bad Cop out of the running, I could probably just ask nicely and Dad would grunt in affirmation and that would be that.

"Oh really?" Dad says. He glances once more at Mom, who seems to be so deeply absorbed in the contemplation of her uneaten salad that she's turning a little green herself.

"Really," I reply.

"That's pretty bold for a girl who just confessed to hitting said Lorelei."

"Isn't it?" I reply, raising my eyebrow and slipping into a slightly British accent. When Dad and I start getting into "English proper," as he calls it, I know I can get whatever I want.

"Quite bold indeed." He murmurs the last word because he's gone back to eating and staring off into space. The debate is over and I've won. Everything feels unnervingly easy tonight.

Mom's chair scrapes against the hardwood as she gets up. The noise is so abrupt that it scares everyone in the room, including JC, who is now wide awake, face contorted into the right-before-crying arrangement. Mom starts clearing the table, even though we're not fully finished eating. Dad and I just sort of watch her and don't say anything. When Mom leaves, he looks over at me. I raise a single eyebrow at him as though to say: *Do you see how weird she's acting?*

"She's been very tired since JC. Giving birth takes a lot out of a person, you know."

At least he's noticed something, but that's only part of the story. I know that Mom and Dad didn't expect to have JC. Mom went back to work as soon as I was old enough to go to full-day school. She loves her job, and she was hoping to become fire chief of her division. She was up for the promotion and I was about to head to high school when she got pregnant. She seemed pretty shocked about it, and for nine whole months she walked around in a daze. It's not that Mom and Dad don't love JC, but surprise babies are obviously tiring. Tiring is one thing though. A missing heart is quite another.

"It's been six months since she had him." I shove as much macaroni as I can into my mouth before Mom comes back.

"Six months isn't very long," he says.

"If's wong enoup por fhe feasons to fhange," I say.

"Swallow your food before you talk, Julie. You'll choke."

I swallow. "It's long enough for the seasons to change, and for Kalid Darzi's voice to hilariously drop two octaves, and for Lorelei to date and break up with a soulless boy and have him go out with someone else."

"When you're young everything takes less time," Dad says. "For adults, time moves differently; it moves slower."

It's a pretty condescending thing to say, and I'm not actually sure it's true. I know certain things affect time, like gravity. Time changes depending on how close you are to the source of a gravitational pull (the centre of the Earth, for example). But I don't think people have their own gravity—not in any substantial way, at least. Planets and black holes and huge things like that have gravity. And even if Dad were correct about time changing, he's got it backwards. According to my limited knowledge of gravity and time, younger people's time would move more slowly because they're technically closer to the centre of the Earth— being shorter than adults in general.

Mom comes back in and continues stacking the dishes. Our hands brush when I pass her my plate and I'm both surprised and not surprised to feel that she's freezing cold. So cold there's the possibility that she was just standing in the kitchen with her hands in the freezer. I try to look in her eyes, but she's watching the plates as though they're her children instead of me and JC, who is now grunting in his basket like a small piglet hungry for scraps.

"Has he been fed yet?" I ask Mom. She decided not to breastfeed JC when he was born because she read somewhere that it was bad for women to breast-feed boy babies because of estrogen or some such thing. I'm not sure if I believe that, but I'm skeptical by nature. Dad says you have to believe something at some point or you'll just go crazy.

Mom shakes her head no and disappears into the kitchen.

"Okay, I guess I'll go up," I say to my dad. But he just makes a small noise of affirmation and continues staring off into nothing, looking like he's about to pass out on the dining-room table. What a pair my parents are tonight.

When I get to my room I call Lorelei from my cellphone. I have to call her on her family's landline because her father is completely old-fashioned and won't let her have a cell.

The phone rings three times and Lorelei's mother picks up.

"Greenwood residence!" she says in her saccharinely chipper way. Maybe it's part of being a pastor's wife—you never know who's going to call with a church emergency.

"Hi, is Lorelei there?" I ask.

"Oh, Julie dahling, is that you?" She says *darling* the same way Lorelei has been saying it lately, which is probably due to the clandestine womanly bonding times that have been happening over there.

"Yes. It's me."

"How are you, dear?"

I nod into the phone. "I'm fine, thank you. How are you?"

"Oh, I'm just splendid."

It seems impossible that she's *always* splendid, but that's what she says every time.

"Great . . . so, is Lorelei there?"

"Of course! Oh! I heard you're coming on Friday for a sleepover! How fun!"

It's as if she inserts an exclamation point into her voice after every three or four words.

"Yes, I'm excited."

"Great! Oh, here she is now!"

Then Lorelei comes on the line, and for a minute there's the sound of two different phones in my ear. Lorelei and I wait until we hear the click of Mrs. Greenwood hanging up. This takes a minute, probably because she's waiting for us to talk, but we stay silent, of course.

"Mother insisted we play Scrabble after dinner. It was torture, but it's worth it for the movies," Lorelei says immediately.

I love the way she launches instantly into conversations, like we never actually stopped talking but just paused for breath. It's the sign of a true best-friendship.

"And I had to wear a long-sleeved shirt at dinner because you bruised me a bit," she continues. It seems unlikely that I *actually* bruised her; she's probably just being dramatic. I hear various clicks in the background. She's probably sitting at her vanity fiddling with her makeup collection. It includes a whole rainbow tray of eyeshadow, at least twenty different shades of lipstick, perfectly matched skin-tone foundation and four different types of mascara, including a blue one that's my personal favourite. How she's allowed so much leeway in the makeup department given her father situation is a mystery to me. Whenever I ask, Lorelei just smiles and says she uses her feminine wiles, which only further reinforces my idea that she should be the femme in our future relationship.

"Sorry," I say. "Dad gave me crap at dinner when I confessed to it."

"You told your parents?" She laughs, but it sounds a bit muffled, probably because she's got the phone tucked under her chin while she applies something or another. I lean back on my bed and stare at the ceiling and try to imagine that I can see through it all the way into her room.

"Yeah."

"Weird . . . okay, so listen, I'm thinking about joining the organizing committee for the Spring Fling. Because this is our first official high-school dance and I want it to be amazing. But I can't do it alone."

I want to tell Lorelei about my mom and everything that happened this afternoon, but I'm worried she'll just think it's too freaky, and I don't want her to be scared of coming over here or anything. So instead I just tell her I'll do the dance committee with her—I love that she always wants to find ways to make life less boring. Then I listen to her ideas for an hour. They range from a black light in the gym vestibule to sneaking booze into the punch. The idea of sneaking alcohol into the school sounds pretty stupid to me, but I don't say anything because I don't want to ruin her obvious excitement. Lorelei doesn't deal well with people raining on her parade. Once, I told her I didn't think it was a good idea to enter the grade-eight fashion show, seeing as she didn't even own a sewing machine. She refused to talk to me for three days. I was devastated, and I'm definitely not going to let that happen again.

Eventually, after she gets bored of talking about the dance and we are both tired, I hear her climb into bed, so I get into bed too. Then we turn off our lights and fall asleep with the phones resting beside our ears, which makes me insanely happy—it's the closest I can get to sleeping next to her until Friday.

My clock says it's past midnight when I wake up to JC screaming in his room. This happens a lot because he's just a tiny baby and babies don't care about proper sleep schedules, but it's always jarring. I check my phone. It hung up at some point while I was asleep, so I've lost my connection to Lorelei. I lie in bed for a little while listening to the baby cry. Then I hear a creak on the old floors and hop out of bed to check on Mom. It's always Mom who takes care of JC at night—Dad wears earplugs so he can get a reasonable amount of sleep and be mentally prepared for work.

And there she is, standing at the top of the stairs with the wailing baby in her arms.

At this point I feel pretty relieved, like I've been holding my breath for hours and I'm finally allowed to exhale. This is normal Mom—comforting JC in the night. I stand there in the hall and watch her for a minute. There's moonlight streaming in from a window and it makes her look sort of silvery and wispy, like she's a ghost woman holding a ghost baby and they both died in the house ages ago and have haunted the halls ever since. She's at the top of the stairs looking down, and suddenly my relief evaporates as I realize her posture looks familiar. It's the same pose she had at dinner when she was holding the macaroni pan. She's looking down at JC like he's a foreign object, and I feel utterly sure she's going to release him from her grasp. The feeling is so strong that panic sets in and I take a step forward and forget to skip a big creaky spot in the floor.

Crrreeeeeaaakkkk.

Mom turns to look at me. Her eyes go wide and JC cries even louder.

"Sorry," I say. My whole body feels tense; I'm still trying to keep quiet, even though I'm totally caught.

"I was going to take him for a ride," she replies, her voice a flat whisper.

Car riding is a thing that calms our family. We all like it. When Mom and Dad are fighting they go for a ride to work it out. When I'm feeling upset Mom takes me driving to calm me down. And when the baby is crying the feeling of the road is the only thing that seems to soothe him. Dad says our family comes from a long line of travellers, so we've got the road in our blood. I'm not sure that's true, but I do know Grandpa Christopher used to work for Chrysler and his job was putting the wheels on the cars. I personally haven't learned to drive yet, but Dad promised me lessons as soon as I turn sixteen so I can carry on our family's proud tradition.

"Okay," I say. "I'm going back to bed then, I guess."

Mom nods and heads down the stairs. I creep back into my room and lie in bed. I listen to the car start and then drive away. I try to breathe deeply to calm myself down, but panic is still pulsing through me. Maybe I should have gone with her?

I'm so worried about it that I can't get back to sleep.

I toss and turn for a while and watch the clock count the minutes.

But I'm too restless, so I get up and throw on my jeans and a hoodie that smells like paint. The last time I wore it was in art when I brushed a line of red across my chest to be funny and pretended I'd been slashed with a knife. This got me a stern lecture from the art teacher, Mr. Francelli, due to the fact that my hijinks made Cal Hawkins have a bit of a meltdown because his brother's girlfriend's aunt was stabbed to death a few months ago. Mr. Francelli said violence was no laughing matter.

Fully dressed, I head out into the hall. I try to avoid the creaks in the floor, even though there's no point because of Dad's earplugs. Still, I miss most of the creaky spots as I make my way down the stairs and out into the street. We live on a quiet side street and it's way past 1:00 a.m., so there's definitely no traffic. I pace up and down beneath the streetlights, on the sidewalk and then on the street. It's been over an hour now. I try to calm my overactive imagination by thinking of Lorelei and our sleepover. I try to conjure up the perfect image of Lorelei sleeping, her face soft and a slight smile curling her lips, but terrible thoughts of fiery car wrecks keep interfering. What if Mom zones out again while she's driving?

To distract myself I decide to walk over to the park. Sometimes Mom takes JC there in his carriage. He's too young to do any of the park activities, like swinging or playing in the sandbox, but she likes him to have some fresh air and to be in the presence of other kids. She calls it pre-socializing. The park isn't far away, a block and a half, but in the quiet night I get a little freaked out. I get even more scared when I notice the park isn't completely abandoned. There's a shadowy figure on the swing set. At first I'm relieved that I've finally found my mom and JC, but then I realize it's only one person. I freeze. I am backing away slowly when I hear my name.

"Julie?"

The shadow from the swing set is moving toward me now and I don't know what to do. My instinct is to run, but I hear my name again and squint toward the shadow.

Short blond hair, soccer shorts, the faint whiff of a familiar cologne.

Ugh. Henry Carter.

He jogs up to me and looks around like he's expecting to see someone else with me.

"What are you doing here?" I ask. I don't mean for it to sound bitchy, but it totally does.

He shrugs. "I come here sometimes."

That's it. As if it's completely normal to be sitting on a swing in a park past 1:00 a.m. on a school night. It's all I can do not to scowl at him.

"What about you?" he asks.

"I was just looking for someone," I say. Then I turn around to leave. I know I'm being rude but I can't help myself. This is the enemy. The guy who took

Lorelei away from me for two whole months. I don't much feel like socializing with him in the middle of the night, all alone.

"Wait," he says.

I turn back to him.

"Do you wanna hang out for a bit?"

"Me?" I ask.

"Who else?" he says, looking around again like he hopes Lorelei might jump out from behind a bush and surprise him.

"Why do you want to hang out with *me*?" I narrow my eyes at him. He probably wants to use me to get to Lorelei. I heard he broke up with Gabriela Souza, and he's probably desperate to get Lorelei back. Just as desperate as I am to have her in the first place.

He looks at me for a long moment and a slight smile tugs at the corners of his lips. Then he shakes his head and shrugs again, only this time it's like he's trying to play it cool. "'Cause you're here," he says.

I roll my eyes. "How flattering."

"No, I didn't mean that. I just . . . " His voice sort of trails off and, for the first time ever, Henry Carter seems awkward and unsure. For a fraction of a second I feel bad for him. What *is* he doing out here so late? Why *does* he want to hang out with me?

Then he straightens up and gives me a cocky half-grin. "Whatever," he says. "Say hi to Lorelei for me, will you?" Without another word he turns around and walks away.

He doesn't look back, and I just watch him leave, confused about what's just happened and trying not to care. Why should I care about stupid Henry Carter and his stupid problems? I have problems of my own. After he rounds the corner and disappears from sight, I make my way back home. I'm flooded with relief when I see my parents' car parked in the driveway. Mom and JC made it home safe. I don't even know why I was worried. Mom was just having a bad day. That's allowed. That's totally allowed.

When I come in the front door, the house is quiet. Mom must already be back in bed, sleeping like a normal person, with a normal soul and a normal heart.

I climb the stairs, deftly avoiding all the creaks, and fall into bed, exhausted and relieved. I don't even bother to take my clothes off. It's past two now and I have to be up for school. At least if I'm dressed when I wake up it's one less thing to do.

3.

My mom took me shopping to pick out my own clothes for the first time when I was three. I wanted her opinion on what I should wear, but she said, "It's important to be your own person." I picked a unicorn sweatshirt and boys' swim trunks. There's a picture and everything. It's embarrassing, but Mom was making an important point.

For obvious reasons I fall asleep in class the next day. When I wake up, all I see is Mr. Gomez's face taking up the entirety of my vision. The rest of the class has left for next period, and Mr. Gomez has pulled a chair up to my desk. His legs are so long I can practically feel them against mine, and his breath smells like cloves, which makes me wistful because it reminds me of making clove oranges for the Christmas tree with Mom. Even though we're not religious or anything, we do celebrate Christmas in the Santa Claus, candy cane, gift-giving way—not the baby Jesus, nativity scene, midnight mass way.

Mr. Gomez's face is so close to mine that it makes me think even more that he might be in love with me, or at least that he wants to kiss me. "I'm worried about you, Jewel-ie," he says, his clove breath washing over me in nostalgic waves. "Talk to me. Is there something going on at home?"

Oh, nothing except my mom told me she doesn't think she has a heart.

"Sorry," I say. "It won't happen again."

He leans forward a little farther and frowns. At this point, I really, really think we're about to kiss, which is interesting because I've never thought about a man (or even a boy) in that way. Ever since I was of the age to have crushes I've been into Lorelei. It's not that I couldn't find a man attractive; it's just that I've never even really considered it in a meaningful way. He puts his hand on mine.

"Maybe I should call your parents?" he asks.

"No, please don't. I'm fine, just a little tired."

Mr. Gomez nods and removes his hand. I almost miss the warm dryness of it. Maybe I shouldn't be closed-minded toward men, even if a teacher having a crush on a student is a little creepy. I leave my hand on the desk in case he wants to touch it again. He smiles and checks his watch, which is a round Rolex with a rim that is the same golden colour as his eyes. Then he stands up just as the bell rings and I hear the shuffling of distant feet in the hall.

"Well, get some sleep tonight, Jewel-ie, because I'll have to contact your parents if you fall asleep in class again."

I smile up at him and open my eyes extra wide to try to look as awake as possible. Then I head out to art class.

Lorelei is in art with me. She spots me as soon as I step in the door and makes a beeline for my desk. She leans over as close as Mr. Gomez did, only her breath smells like bubble gum and I definitely know I want to kiss her, whereas with Mr. Gomez I was on the fence.

"What did *he* say to you?" she asks.

I shrug and try to look super casual. "Well, I fell asleep, which was a pretty dumb move. He was worried, that's all."

I don't know why I'm not telling her about the hand-holding and the almost-leg-touching. She leans over even farther, until our noses are practically rubbing. Then she narrows her eyes like she's trying to read a particularly hard-to-understand sentence.

"That's it?" she asks.

"Yeah," I reply.

She pulls away and smiles. Then she does her hair-flippy thing and slides into the desk next to me as Mr.

Francelli starts handing out the paints. I'm not allowed to have red anymore, thanks to the whole painted hoodie/pretend blood incident that sent Cal Hawkins home in hysterics.

After art it's lunch, and Lorelei and I eat together in the yard, although I have to wait while she talks to practically everyone in the hall on the way out. It's always awkward when that happens. I'm not friends with as many people as she is, so I basically just stand around beside her and wait for her conversations to end.

Over lunch I listen while she tells me more about her plans for the Spring Fling. The first committee meeting is this afternoon, right after school on the gym stage. I'm kind of relieved; it means I won't be getting home until later, hopefully when Dad is already there and I won't have to deal with any after-school Mom weirdness.

While Lorelei is talking we're interrupted by Henry, who kicks a soccer ball under our picnic table, probably on purpose. He struts over like a peacock, his athletic legs flexing in the sunshine. He's completely back to his old self now—no more awkward pauses like in the park. He gives Lorelei a long, amorous look and his eyes flicker over to me for the briefest of seconds before he crawls under the table. He brushes against Lorelei's leg as he grabs the ball.

"Hi, Lorelei," he says, once he's out from under the table.

"Hi, Henry." Lorelei rolls her eyes in a dramatic way.

"Hi, Julie," he says.

This shocks me. It seems to shock Lorelei too, because she opens her mouth and closes it again quickly, like she was going to say something but couldn't think of the words. Lorelei isn't used to me getting any attention, and honestly, neither am I.

"Hi," I say quietly.

"You going to the dance?" Henry says, this time to Lorelei, as he juts his hip out and balances all of his weight on one foot, resting the ball on his side like it's a baby.

"I'm *planning* the dance," Lorelei says.

Henry grins. "Are you gonna wear the red dress?"

Lorelei rolls her eyes again. "In your dreams, Henry."

I hold my breath, both to avoid the smell of Henry's cologne and because I know he could, at any moment, ask Lorelei to the dance.

"Maybe I'll see you there," he says. I exhale and look over at Lorelei. Her face is impassive, and I'm relieved.

Henry smiles. His eyes pass over me and pause for a second before he lets the ball drop to the ground. It bounces and he kicks it in the air a couple of times, real pro style, then runs off kicking.

"See what I'm saying, Julie? *So* immature. We didn't even get to third base and he thinks he has the right to tell me what to wear!" She flicks a tomato off her salad and it falls to the dirt.

I do my best to close my gaping mouth before Lorelei looks my way. The fact that she and Henry got to *second base* is news to me. I thought they only went as far as making out.

"Don't look so shocked, Julie. I didn't want to tell you because I thought you'd make a big deal out of it, but it's really not a big deal at all. Practically everyone's done it," Lorelei says. She's speaking super fast, so I can tell she feels guilty about not having told me in the first place.

"Not everyone's doing it. *I* haven't done it," I say. It sounds lame—by grade nine you are at least expected to have had your first kiss—but I've loved Lorelei since I was nine years old, and it's honestly never occurred to me to kiss anyone else.

"Well, it was no big deal," she says as she continues to pick at her salad and flick tomatoes onto the ground, much to the delight of the schoolyard ant community.

"What was it like? Second base . . . ," I ask, leaning in. It's a question I'd really like to ask Henry, but I can't, for obvious reasons.

She sighs in her lovely way and combs her hair with her fingers as she looks into the distance that people look into when they're trying to remember the past. "Soft, warm, exciting. He was a good kisser too, so I guess that's something."

"Wow," I say, "I guess I wouldn't know what a good kisser is . . . "

She looks at me, her brow furrowed into delicate little folds. "I can't believe you've never kissed anyone before."

I make a sad face and lean in a little closer, hoping this will serve as the invitation needed to progress to the next level.

She smiles and reaches out to touch my cheek. "You are such a perfect innocent, dahling," she whispers. Our faces are close, and I can practically feel the ridges of her fingerprints on my cheeks. My stomach is doing somersaults and my breath is coming in short, painful pulses. But, of course, at that moment—just as she's looking pensive on the subject of me and kissing—the bell rings and a wave of chattering kids run by and ruin the mood completely.

"English," she says. Then she packs up her salad and her dance committee notes and I straggle behind her as we make our way back to class.

. . .

After English it's math, which means test review. I managed to study a bit at home, but there has been so much stress and weirdness going on I can't say I'm fully ready. At least I get to share most of my classes with Lorelei. Once in a while I look up from my work to watch her. She's studying her notes closely. I know she has a bit of trouble with math sometimes, but she still acts confident about it, despite a couple of low test scores. Dad once described Mom as *lyrical*, and I liked the way that sounded. That's how Lorelei is; she has a lyrical way of moving that makes her look like she's always singing a song, or maybe having a song sung about her. I even tried to write a song about her once, but I only got as far as "Lorelei, you make my heart burn" before I ripped up the pages and put a match to them. Of course Mom got really mad that I started a small fire in my garbage can, but it was worth losing TV privileges for a week and listening to her whole fire-safety school presentation to see my sad attempt at songwriting go up in flames.

After math it's world issues with Mr. Gomez. This term we're doing United Nations, which is this simulation where everyone takes a UN country and we debate stuff and try to solve problems. I got the Democratic Republic of the Congo assigned to me because I was sick on the day everyone got to pick countries. I feel a little overwhelmed by the whole

UN thing though. There are so many problems in the world that it's impossible for a bunch of smart *adults* to solve them, never mind a classroom full of ninth graders. The debate is lively today because France keeps fighting with Pakistan about banning the niqāb in public places, and Mr. Gomez keeps throwing out questions about freedom of expression, and freedom of religion versus national security.

"Everyone has the right to wear what they want, to do what they want with their bodies," says Pakistan.

"It's a matter of security. We have to be able to see who people are. We have to see their expressions to really trust them," France counters.

"It's a ridiculous human rights infringement," Switzerland pipes up. "And to suggest that we can't extend trust to people based on their appearance leads to a place I'm not sure you want to go." Switzerland shoots France a serious look and France scowls at the entire UN.

I'm quiet because I'm not quite sure where I stand on the whole thing. Congo doesn't have an opinion on it, as far as I know. But I do know that it takes all kinds to make a world, so I'm not sure France is on particularly solid ground.

When the bell rings everyone slaps their binders closed. Thirty chairs scrape and sixty feet shuffle and soon it's just me and Lorelei and Mr. Gomez left in the room. I pack up my stuff and try to avoid eye contact with Mr. Gomez as he cleans the blackboard. Lorelei packs her stuff too and whistles something I don't recognize because she's so off-key. She waits by my desk and we hold hands as we go out.

Halfway down the hall she stops short. "I forgot my dance notes. You go on ahead and meet me in the gym," she says. Then she turns and runs back down the hall toward the classroom. I wish I had gone with her. I hate when she runs off and leaves me alone, especially because the dance is *her* thing.

I linger by the gym door and wait for Lorelei while a handful of other kids and the gym teacher, Mrs. Singh, trickle in. I'm glad it's Mrs. Singh who's running the committee and not the principal, Mr. Lynch, because Mrs. Singh is beautiful and soft whereas Mr. Lynch is ugly and hard. I realize this is shallow reasoning, but I do have my preferences.

Lorelei arrives last. She bursts through the door dramatically, her smooth cheeks tinted a luscious pink from running.

"Sorry I'm late, dahling."

"Welcome to the dance committee," Mrs. Singh says to each of us as we climb onto the stage. We mill about and pour ourselves some OJ and grab a cookie from the centre of the half-circle before sitting cross-legged on the hardwood. I guess committee life isn't all that bad if they're willing to feed us.

Josie Khan and Carla Reyes are there, which is pretty

exciting because I'm hoping we'll become friends and I can grill them about their kissing practice. Then there's me and Lorelei, of course, and finally this guy named Ed Simpson who everyone thinks is gay and possibly dating a grade twelve from the all-boys school up the street. I'm surprised there aren't any grade twelves on the committee, but I guess they're all too busy planning their senior prom to be bothered with the Spring Fling. We go around the semicircle and introduce ourselves, even though we all know each other, for the most part. Then Mrs. Singh tells us she'll be in her office if we need her, but that the theme, decorations, posters and snacks for the dance are all up to us. That's it. No more teacher wisdom, just the expectation of independence. The joys of high-school maturity.

Everyone's pretty quiet for a couple of minutes after Mrs. Singh leaves, eating cookies and talking softly amongst themselves. I try to angle myself toward Josie and Carla, but they don't really pay any attention to me. Eventually Lorelei stands up and drags me with her to centre stage. She pulls out her notes and takes charge.

"So, here's what's happening," Lorelei says. "This is my first high-school formal and I want it to be unforgettable, so I have a list of ways to make this perfect . . . " She waves her list in the air and every eye on the stage follows the motion of it.

Josie and Carla look a bit miffed that Lorelei is taking control, but as soon as Lorelei whispers that she wants to sneak booze into the punch their frowns turn into smiles. I can't say I support the plan though. Is it really the best idea to get a bunch of teenagers drunk when we'll be surrounded by teachers all night? It feels a bit stupid to me. But everyone else seems into it, so I keep my thoughts to myself.

"Okay, let's talk about theme," Lorelei says. "I'm thinking Sugar 'n' Spice."

Ed rolls his eyes. "That's a little twee, don't you think?" he asks. But he's not even looking at Lorelei; his eyes are glued to his phone. He seems to have been in a non-stop text conversation this whole time—maybe with his grade-twelve BF?

A shadow of a frown passes over Lorelei's face. Then she cocks her head to the side and eyes Ed. "Well, do you have any better ideas?"

"What about Enchantment Under the Sea? *Back to the Future* styles," he says, again not even bothering to look up.

"Ugh, *Back to the Future*? Are you kidding?" Lorelei asks.

"It would be totally retro," Ed continues, finally looking up from his phone and grinning.

"What's *Back to the Future*?" Josie asks.

"Seriously?" Ed says, rolling his eyes again.

"Too obscure." Lorelei shoots me a look like she wants me to say something.

"Uh . . . I like Sugar 'n' Spice," I say.

Ed laughs and shakes his head, his attention dropping once again to his phone.

"Me too," Josie replies.

"Good, then it's settled. Majority rules," Lorelei says quickly, not even bothering to get Carla's opinion.

"Whatever," Ed says. He sounds kind of annoyed, but he doesn't push it.

The rest of the hour passes quickly. I mostly just gorge myself on juice and cookies, nod at everything Lorelei says and try not to stare too hard at Josie and Carla. By the time the meeting is over Lorelei has assigned everyone a task (mine being poster design—because I've been working on my graphics skills at the computer lab and a bit at home too and I must admit I'm not terrible at it) and we nail down the Sugar 'n' Spice theme—we agree to encourage everyone to dress either really cute or really sexy. I can guess which dress style everyone will choose though. Nobody wants to be the cute one at a high-school dance.

At 4:30 on the dot Mrs. Singh comes out of the office to check on us and says, "I'm so impressed that you're so organized! This is really well done."

Lorelei beams at this compliment, of course.

On the way home I try to walk extra slowly, even

though Lorelei is rushing ahead after all the excitement of dance planning.

"Maybe event planning is my calling," she says. "Can you even think of a better career choice? I could be one of those event planners to the stars. Big lavish parties with champagne fountains and everyone having sex with everyone else's wife . . . "

I think she's actually talking about a swinger party, but I don't mention it. Her excitement is infectious and her hair bounces and catches the dying light of the sun in this really beautiful way that makes me want to kiss her way more than I've ever wanted to kiss her before.

"So . . . I'm excited about our sleepover tomorrow," I say after her planning high has died down a bit.

"Oh, for sure. We have that game and some movies and Mother says she'll stay out of our hair."

"Maybe you could tell me more about you and Henry . . . and what kissing him was like," I say.

She laughs. "What, are you hot for Henry or something?"

"No, I just . . . it's just that I haven't kissed anyone before and I want to know what it's like." I hope I'm not laying it on too thick.

"I've had better than Henry." She shrugs, and I don't know what to say. Who else has she kissed? I search my memory for all the times she's said the words *kiss* or *make out*, but I can't remember. And

I pay extra attention when she talks about that kind of stuff.

"Who else have you kissed?" I ask.

She's wearing her cat-eye sunglasses and she laughs again, throwing her head back in this way that makes it look like she's about to eat the sun. "I don't know . . . a bunch of people," she says.

I can't go any slower and soon we're at my front door. Then Lorelei leans over so her mouth is right above my ear and says, "Maybe I'll let you practise on me tomorrow, and I'll teach you how Henry likes it."

At this point I'm frozen in place. She pulls away and kisses both my cheeks like they do in France. Each cheek holds the electric imprint of her lips, and the sizzle of it travels all the way down to my toes. Then she giggles and sweeps down my walkway in the most lyrical fashion yet. My stomach is clenching and unclenching in a not particularly unpleasant way as I watch her go. I can feel my heartbeat up in my eyeballs. I want to jump and dance and holler at the sky, but I try to keep my composure in case she turns back and sees me. Her breath is still caught in the deepest part of my ear, and her words are still rattling around in there—where I hope they will stay all night and all day tomorrow until we're finally alone in her room and I can remind her of exactly what she said. I take a few deep breaths and try to hold on to the scent of her shampoo; it always lingers a bit after she's gone.

Everything changes when I walk in the front door. All the lightness drains from my body and it feels like there isn't enough oxygen in the hall. There is noticeably less once I get to the dining room, where JC is in his basket, Dad is at the table on his laptop and Mom is off somewhere in the kitchen being thin and barely there.

"Hi," I say as I drop my backpack and slide into my seat.

"Hi, honey," Dad says tiredly. "How was school?" He looks up from his laptop for a fraction of a second before refocusing on the screen.

Amazing. I'm going to kiss the girl I've loved for basically my whole life and I can't wait. I wish I had a time machine so I could travel all the way to tomorrow and not wait another second. "We were planning for the Spring Fling," I say.

"Hmm . . . gotta date?"

"Naw, I'm just going with Lorelei." *The woman I love. Who, did I mention, I'm going to kiss tomorrow.*

I lean back in my chair. I'm trying to be casual but the stupid thing creaks loudly and Dad looks up at me.

"Did you fart?" he asks.

I laugh. "No . . . did you?"

That's our little game on these old creaky chairs

in this old creaky house. For a second I allow myself to believe that everything is normal. But that second passes when Mom comes in from the kitchen holding JC's bottle. She looks tired and empty. Her hair is an unkempt pile of dead leaves, and there's still that hunch to her shoulders that suggests she's carrying something invisible but very heavy on her back. She doesn't make eye contact with me. She just moves quietly over to JC's basket and scoops him out to feed him. I look over at Dad but he's oblivious, lost in his work.

"You look tired," I say, each word loud and conspicuous. I'm talking to Mom but looking at Dad. He looks up from his screen for a second to inspect Mom.

"You should go get a massage on Saturday and I'll watch the kids," Dad says. As if that settles it. As if all of Mom's troubles will melt away under the capable hands of some woman named Anna who uses different-coloured crystals for healing different types of illnesses and always smells faintly of sage. Mom nods vaguely and slips back into the kitchen with JC while Dad grunts his "that's settled then" grunt and goes back to his work.

I pull out some homework, but I can barely focus because I'm so full of excitement and stress. My cheeks are still on fire from Lorelei's kisses and I can't believe that soon my lips will be too.

• • •

JC is screaming again; he's such a night owl. His cries crawl along the hall and squeeze under the crack in my door, past Lorelei's words still ringing in my ears. But this time I don't hear the creak of the floorboards telling me Mom is taking JC for a ride. I just hear JC, wailing like he's the most miserable baby that ever was. Although I would rather stay in bed and dream of Lorelei's lips, after five minutes I can't take it anymore, so I get out of bed and sneak into the hall. I listen for the sound of JC's baby voice coming from my parents' room, but instead I hear his cries snaking up from downstairs. My heart jumps into my throat. What is he doing down there? Where's Mom? Is she off in the kitchen being weird again?

I make my way downstairs cautiously and follow the sound of JC to the parlour. The room is dimly lit by the streetlight that's shining straight in through the window. JC is in his basket, and I quickly scoop him up and bounce him up and down to shush him. He calms down pretty quickly because he's a good baby, and I hum a bit of some random tune, which he seems to like. Then I spot something on the coffee table.

A sheet?

No, a lumpy sheet.

No, a sheet with a face and other human appendages.

Every part of me goes cold. Goosebumps rise on my arms and my throat dries up.

"Mom?" I whisper. I can barely make the word come out properly, I'm so scared.

She doesn't respond.

She's barely breathing, but I can see a teensy bit of a rise and fall beneath the bedsheet. And here I am again, JC cradled in my arms, stepping closer to my unresponsive, creepy mother.

"Mom?" I say again. I lean over and squeeze her shoulder. I know she can hear me, but I can't bring myself to say anything else other than "Mom." Everything feels like it's back on the edge of normal, and I don't want to be the one to kick it off.

I see the impression of her eyes opening under the sheet, although it's probably hard for her to see anything because it's one of Dad's thousand-thread-count Egyptian cotton sheets.

"Mom." I try a different tone to see if I can get a response.

Then Mom sits up, but she doesn't move. Two little tears rise up and squeeze out of the side of each of my eyes. JC is squirming in my arms as I reach out a shaky hand and pull the sheet off. Underneath, Mom is a pale paste with two black smudges under her eyes. I know she's been tired lately and baggy-eyed, but this is a new level of pallid that makes my breath catch in my throat.

"What the hell are you doing?" I ask.

Is she pretending to be dead or something? People

don't just lie around under white sheets—unless they're corpses.

"My heart is gone," she whispers.

I want to scream, to shake her, to cry. But instead I just stand there dumbly and stare at her. She's not looking at me; she's just looking straight ahead, like there's something important she forgot and she's trying to remember it.

"You taught me how to feel for a pulse a couple years ago, do you remember?" I ask.

She nods, and I reach out with my free hand to grab her arm. I use my index and middle fingers and slide them around on her wrist until I find her pulse.

"See, it's there," I say, urgently. "That means your heart is beating."

I take her other hand and place her fingers on her wrist, over her pulse.

"See? Your heart," I say.

She shakes her head a little, then turns to look at me. Her face softens and I see a shadow of a smile on her lips.

"Of course," she says. "My heart. Sorry."

I take a deep, shaky breath. "Mom. What's going on?" I ask.

JC is still squirming on my hip, holding his arms out toward Mom like he's starving and she's a bottle full of milk.

"Nothing. I just . . . I was just resting," she says.

"No one just rests under a sheet like that, Mom. Unless they're dead."

"Dead," she whispers.

JC starts to gurgle and cries a little louder. So I take the sheet off Mom's lap and put it on the floor, then hand her the baby. She looks down at him with an empty expression. She doesn't even bounce him or anything, but he immediately quiets in her arms.

"Well, you're not dead. You're very much alive, and you should go to bed," I say. "And maybe we should talk to Dad about this in the morning?"

"No." She shakes her head like she's just woken up and is trying to dispel a bad dream. "No. Max is so busy . . . this is our secret, remember?" Her voice is pleading, almost normal, and she looks me right in the eyes. Her eyes are like two big question marks asking: *Will you keep my secret?*

"But I really think . . . "

"Julie, please. I need you to help me—and your dad."

Is it really about helping my dad, or is there something else going on between them?

"Okay," I say, reluctantly. Having her say my name makes me feel better for some reason. Like, if she knows who I am, somehow everything will be all right.

"Thank you. Everything will be fine. Let's just go to bed."

I help her off the table and she leans against me hard for a second, like she can't stand on her own. And we just stand there for a few minutes, side by side with the streetlight streaming through the window and the bedsheet lying on the ground like a crumpled ghost.

After a while she starts to move, and I follow her out of the parlour, toward the stairs.

"Are you okay now?" I ask, even though I know the answer can't possibly be yes.

"Okay," she replies quietly. As if that's a real answer.

4.

I started kindergarten when I was four. We have this picture of me and my mom in the schoolyard on my first day. I'm wearing these little blue overalls and holding my mom's hand. I'm not looking at the camera or smiling or anything, I'm just looking up at my mom with a worried expression on my face. If I close my eyes I can bring myself back there. She was so warm and solid beside me. I didn't want her to leave.

I barely sleep after Mom's little episode. The sun hasn't come up yet and all I can hear are a few birds. I try to distract myself from my troubles by replaying the scene with Lorelei over and over in my mind—those words, *practise* and *me*, at the epicentre of my imaginings. Despite the Mom mess, I haven't been this hyped since the Christmas when I was six and I stayed up all night and puked a couple of times because I was so excited about presents. I'm pretty sure I'm not going to puke now, but I'm not denying the possibility.

Finally, at 6:00 a.m. I hear Dad creaking in the hall and I give myself permission to at least get up and try on every outfit I own. I opt for the most boyish ensemble I can because I'm still banking on the butch/femme thing. I really think I'm the best candidate for the manly one in the relationship: my hair is not only way shorter than Lorelei's, but also I don't care about stuff like makeup or dresses or beauty products of any kind, really.

I don't want to have breakfast with Mom and see her puffy eyes and pale face so I just pack my overnight bag and run downstairs.

"I'm going to Lorelei's tonight, so I won't be back till tomorrow!" I say as I'm passing by the dining room, where Dad is standing in his boxers drinking coffee.

"Bye!" Dad says. That's the last thing I hear because I've already slammed the front door and I'm on my way down the street.

It's still super early—like 7:00 a.m. early—so I head over to the Starbucks four blocks away from school and order a double-whip caramel macchiato and a blueberry scone. Then I worry last-minute about bad breath so I buy one of those tins of way-too-expensive mints as well. The barista pauses before she rings up my order and squints down at me like she's thinking, *This kid is too young for coffee; it will stunt her growth*. But then she just shrugs and takes my money. What does she care about my growth anyway?

I sit on a tall stool and watch people walk by. I think about my mom under that bedsheet on the coffee table. What the hell was she thinking? I know she's been tired because of JC, and there's obviously something weird going on between her and Dad, but this is too much. I don't like keeping it a secret from my dad, but I don't want to betray her. She trusts me to keep this to myself, so that's what I'm going to do. I try to push the image of her body outlined in the white sheet from my mind. Try to replace it with Lorelei: her beautiful flowing hair wrapped around me, her fingers entwined with mine, her lips and mine pressed together, our bodies so close I can feel the heat of her.

Then I see Henry.

And he sees me.

Crap.

He gives me a little wave and comes into the Starbucks. I try to pretend I'm really focused on my caramel macchiato while I watch him out of the corner of my eye. He talks to the barista and I think I see her laugh. How charming. I take a big bite of my blueberry scone as he comes up behind me. Maybe if he sees me with my mouth full he'll just keep on walking.

"Hi," he says.

No such luck.

"Hi," I say, and a big piece of scone flies out of my

mouth and hits the window. I try to contain my blush and hold my hand to my mouth while I swallow.

Henry slips onto the stool beside me. Completely uninvited. I notice his soccer shorts have a bit of dirt on them, like he just finished a game, even though it's not even 8:00 a.m. Do they actually have soccer practice that early? Do I even care?

He shakes his espresso-type frozen drink and it sloshes against the sides of the cup. "Liquid energy."

I try really hard not to groan.

We're silent for a long time then. It's so awkward. I try not to look at him, but I keep seeing him at the edge of my vision. His blond hair reminds me of Lorelei, and I close my eyes for a moment and try to focus on the sound of her voice, still caught in my ear canal. *I'll let you practise on me.*

"So, are *you* going to the dance?" Henry asks, jarring me out of my lovely daydream.

"Why?" I ask as dismissively as possible. I don't understand why he's talking to me, and I really don't need this right now.

"I just thought . . . maybe you and Lorelei would be going together," he says. He drank his coffee really quickly and now he's sucking at the bit at the bottom and it's making this horrible squelching sound.

"Look, I don't know why you care what Lorelei or I do. I mean, didn't she break up with you?" I ask.

He looks stricken, and for a second I feel guilty for rubbing it in. If Lorelei had broken up with me, I wouldn't want someone shoving it in my face.

"Sorry," I offer.

He nods. "It's fine. I guess I'm just trying to make conversation."

"Why?" I ask. Only this time I'm more curious than rude.

He sighs. "I just . . . well, we keep bumping into each other, so why not?"

I don't have a good answer, really. I guess I could try to be civil.

"Are *you* going to the dance?" I ask.

He turns his whole body to face me, stays like that for a long moment, and then just shrugs and looks at his watch. "We're gonna be late," he says.

I shove the last bit of scone in my mouth and slip off my stool. We walk over to the school together in silence and part at the front door with nothing but a small wave.

After school, Lorelei and I walk hand in hand back to her house while she talks about the dance committee. I look at her profile against the afternoon sun. I haven't mentioned kissing practice all day, but I think at some point I should bring it up so she doesn't forget. I don't know why she would have suggested it in the first place if she wasn't into it, but since she doesn't officially know how I feel about her it's possible she's never really thought about me *like that.*

So tonight the plan is: kissing practice, then tell Lorelei how I feel. Kissing first is key though. I need to gauge the intensity of her feelings for me through the barometer of her lips.

"So how's the poster coming?" Lorelei asks.

"Um, well, I'm still conceptualizing it," I reply. The truth is I haven't really had much time to think about it, with all the stuff going on at home. But I will—soon.

"I'm sure you'll conceptualize the hell out of it," she says. Can she even say *hell*? Isn't that verboten in the world of Anglicans? I guess kissing your girl best friend is probably also against the religious law, so maybe she just isn't really an Anglican. It's not like she has to believe in the same religion as her father just because he's a pastor. Now that I think about it, even though we've been best friends since grade three, I don't *actually know* if she believes in God. We don't really talk about stuff like that.

"Do you believe in God?" I ask.

She drops my hand and stops walking to look at me.

"Out of nowhere much?" she says.

"Sorry. It's just, your dad is a pastor and I just

thought maybe, but if you don't want to talk about it . . . "

She's standing in front of the sun and her face is in shadow; a thick golden halo rises around her head. Was that the wrong question? Have I messed everything up?

She smiles. "Church is kind of cool, I guess, because you get to drink wine."

"Oh." I can't imagine her at church, even though I know she goes every weekend with her parents.

"Funerals are okay too, because you get free food and there's always a bunch of little old ladies who bake these amazing cakes and pies and stuff . . . "

All of my insides tighten when she says the word *funeral*. The last thing I want to think about right now is my mom, but the image of her still body under the bedsheet floats across my vision. I do my best to ignore it.

"Actually," she continues, "there's a funeral next Friday. You wanna go?"

I laugh nervously and shrug.

"Come on, it'll be fun. Sometimes there's an open casket and you can actually see the corpse." Lorelei grabs my hand again and we keep going down the street, past my house and around the corner. I glance at my window, to see if I can see my mom in the parlour. Is she back under the sheet on the table? The light is hitting the window in a way that makes the inside invisible though, so I see nothing but my reflection, paired with Lorelei's.

"That's morbid," I say.

"Not really. I mean, everyone says the dead go on to a better place, like heaven, so whatever."

We climb the stairs of her front porch and the wood doesn't make a sound. It looks brand new, freshly painted.

"But do you think they are? Going somewhere better?" I ask.

She shrugs again and tosses her hair around. "Who cares? The food is worth it, trust me." She throws herself against the door, opens it, and the smell of turkey and roasting potatoes hits my nose.

Lorelei's house is the polar opposite of mine; where mine is dark and creaky, hers is bright and silent, padded with this creamy beige carpet that looks like sponge toffee. Every surface in her house gleams and smells like lemon, and her mother looks like a housewife from another time. Mrs. Greenwood greets us with a smile that's like saying *hi* and *welcome* and *mi casa es su casa* all at the same time. I feel an ache in my chest as she pulls me into this massive mom-sized hug and I inhale her lemony/turkey/hairspray scent. She's so mom-like. So normal it makes me jealous. Once I overheard Megan Ling telling our English teacher,

Mrs. Sinclair, that her mother was in rehab; it spread pretty quickly around the school. I felt bad for Megan but I also felt relieved that I had a normal mother. Not anymore.

"It's been so long, dahling," she says.

"Hi, Mrs. Greenwood," I reply, but my words come out a bit muffled because I'm literally buried in her bosom.

Lorelei rolls her eyes and drags me through the fresh, bright, quiet house to her room, which is practically made of the colour yellow. Seriously: yellow throw pillows, comforter, walls, desk, vanity, carpet. It's a room that you couldn't be sad in if you tried. Lorelei throws down her backpack and puts on some Miley. Then she starts pulling out the entire contents of her closet and putting all the clothes on her bed. I sit down beside a pile of miniskirts and watch her.

"I've been looking at you all day," she says.

My heart thunks so hard I can feel it in my throat.

"We have got to find you something more girly, because you'll never capture Henry's attention in that . . . " She tosses a hand toward me as though she's trying to encompass all of me with a single gesture. So much for butch and femme.

"I don't care about Henry," I say.

She laughs. "*Everyone* cares about Henry."

"Even you?"

68

She continues to yank clothes off hangers and pile them beside me. The heap is getting so big I can barely see her anymore, so I slide off the bed and sit on the floor.

"Don't be silly," she says. "I like older men. I told you I have mature tastes."

I lean back against her bed and stretch my legs out along the carpet, trying my hardest to look completely and totally at ease. "What kind of older men?"

"This is about you and Henry, dahling, not me and my conquests," she replies, smiling at me.

I want to ask about her conquests, but this is my opportunity and there's no way I'm not going to take it. "Well, I've never even kissed anybody before, so I wouldn't know what to do with him if I had him."

There, I said it.

I hold my breath as she freezes for a second with her back to me. My heart is definitely going to come out through my throat at any moment.

"Right," she says. Then she turns around gracefully and prances over to me. She drops to her knees beside me, grabs my face and puts her lips on mine.

Her mouth tastes like lipstick and her lips are softer than anything I've ever felt before. I feel little explosive bursts where her bottom lip touches mine and the sparks travel through my blood straight into my brain, making me feel light-headed. My heart is blowing up, pounding faster than anything I've ever felt, and I feel the heat of Lorelei's hands, pressing into my shoulders. I'm giddy with pleasure and there's nothing I could compare this to even if I was in the state of mind to be comparing anything to anything. I'm so excited I can't even breathe, and I wish I could be in the moment but I know the moment will be gone so quickly that I spend most of the short kiss wishing I could do something to make it longer. I wrap my arms around her waist and pull her into me. She gives a guttural little yelp that reverberates against my lips. Every part of me is on fire and I want it to last forever. But after a couple more seconds Lorelei pulls away and hops up. My arms stay out in front of me for a moment, like they're still holding onto her. She doesn't even look at me; she just goes back to pulling clothes out of her closet.

"The trick with Henry," she says, "is that he likes when you take the initiative. He acts all tough at school and he struts and preens and all that, but he's kind of soft and he doesn't really like to be in charge."

I nod, but all I'm thinking about is her lips. The electricity is still pulsing through me. "Oh," I say, because I figure I have to say something.

Then I hear a snippet of the techno version of Beethoven's Fifth Symphony, which is Lorelei's favourite— the symphony, not the techno. Lorelei runs to her backpack and digs around.

"Shit," she says, "I forgot to put it on vibrate."

I've never heard her say *shit* before, and I didn't know she had a cellphone either—she always told me her father wouldn't allow it. But I don't really care, because I'm still feeling her hands on my shoulders, my hands on her waist.

She looks at the screen and narrows her eyes.

"It's Henry," she says.

She quickly types something, the little clicking noises of the keys going a mile a minute.

Henry is texting on a private, unknown cellphone. I shuffle over to lean against the wall beside the closet in an effort to get a look at the screen. I can feel a thick blush staining my cheeks as I try to peek over her shoulder.

Then another snippet of Beethoven's Fifth, but she quickly flips the switch on the side of the phone to silence it.

"Oh God." Lorelei sighs, rolls her eyes and flips her hair—an awesome display of angsty exasperation. I lean over farther to try to get a look at what she's typing, but she's too far away; I can't see the words. She keeps typing for another couple of seconds, switches off the phone, then takes a flying leap at the pile of clothes on her bed. She lands lightly on top and crosses her legs. I slither off the floor and sit on the bed at the bottom of the pile, looking up at her. All I want to do is climb up there and pull her down on top of me, but I don't know if she would like that or if she would just get all freaked out. I'm frozen with uncertainty.

"You have a cellphone?" I ask. I'm trying not to sound flummoxed or angry or judgy.

"Yeah, but don't tell. I bought it at the beginning of grade nine. So yeah, that was Henry . . . "

"Why didn't you tell me?"

She shrugs and laughs. "Because you're allowed to call here anytime and no one cares."

"So Henry texts a lot?"

"You're jealous!" she says.

"I am not," I say. But I am, obviously—totally jealous. I can still feel her lips on mine and I don't want to talk about Henry right now. I would do anything to get her back in front of me, the entire warmth of her leaning in, her breath all I can breathe.

"Don't worry, we're not an item anymore. He's all yours."

I shrug and lie back on her pillow. It smells like her shampoo—I adore that smell. I take a deep breath. "So what did he want?"

She rolls off the clothes pile and stretches out next to me. We've lain like this a thousand times, side by side at sleepovers. But now it seems more meaningful, tense and full of possibility. I roll over so my whole body is facing her.

"He's going to this party Jamal Williams is having tonight. Jamal's parents are gone and his brother's taking care of him," she says. "I don't know who's going, but it might be cool. It might especially be cool because Jamal's brother is kind of cute—and nineteen—which is definitely better than fifteen."

"Will your parents let us go?" I ask.

She laughs. "Not in a million years, dahling . . . but see that tree out there?" She points out the yellow-framed window to the giant maple outside.

I guess I shouldn't be surprised. "Have you done that before?" I ask.

She turns onto her side, then grabs my waist and pulls me close. I smell her lipstick and her slightly sweet breath. I take big, huge gulps, like she's providing all of my oxygen. Is this it? Are we going to kiss again? I've never prayed before, but I am definitely praying for that.

"Maybe you and Henry can hook up tonight," she says. "Actually, I'll see to it that you do."

"I . . . "

She holds a finger to my lips. "Life is short, Julie. You have to take risks from time to time."

I purse my lips to maximize contact with her finger. Maybe if I'm completely still she won't move either and we can lie like this all night, forget about the stupid party and stupid Henry Carter. Life is short, and I would rather fill my time with moments like this. With her.

But Lorelei shifts, moves her finger away from my lips. "You can wear my miniskirt. You'll look hot," she says. I shiver with pleasure. That's basically all I want in the world right now: for Lorelei to think I'm hot.

"Juuuulie . . . Loooorelei . . . Dinnnnnneeerrr!" It's Mrs. Greenwood calling. Lorelei sits up quickly, crawls across me and runs out the door before I can say another word.

Dinner is steaming on the table when we arrive. It looks like a page plucked from one of those extra-shiny magazines with pictures of rich people's houses and super-fancy gourmet meals in them. I try not to think about my parents at home in the dining room: Mom hesitating by the door with a pan of something hot in her hands, Dad's face buried in his work, not noticing that Mom is missing her heart.

"Hi, Julie, so good to see you! Do you want to say grace?" Pastor Greenwood says. He looks like the perfect partner for Mrs. Greenwood: a plump and old-ish handsome guy with these little round glasses that make him look scholarly and all-knowing. For some reason they love it when I say grace. Lorelei kicks me under the table and gives me a big forced smile.

"Sure . . . um . . . thank you, Pastor and Mrs. Greenwood . . . and God . . . for the delicious-looking food. We think it's fabulous that you, God, made a planet where such delicious things grow. I hope everyone else in the world is blessed with such great food tonight. Amen?"

Mrs. Greenwood laughs and claps and Pastor Greenwood chuckles. Then I realize why they like it when I say grace—because I'm terrible at it. So embarrassing.

We all dig in. Lorelei hoovers her food and talks the whole time—even with her mouth full—about the Spring Fling and the planning committee. She tells her parents that I'm designing the poster and everyone looks at me approvingly. But I can't stop looking at Lorelei's mouth—even with it full of food I want to kiss her again, and kiss her and kiss her and never stop kissing her.

"Julie wants to go to the funeral on Friday," Lorelei says, dishing herself out a third helping of turkey. Ugh, the funeral again. I wish she would drop it, forget all about it. I don't want to go to the stupid, morbid funeral and sit there while some person lies in a coffin, all still and dead with no heartbeat.

Pastor Greenwood looks surprised, his eyebrows rising up over his glasses. "Really?"

I smile and try to look like I'm into it. "I've never been and Lorelei says it's . . . interesting."

"Larry does an excellent eulogy," Mrs. Greenwood says, beaming. "You're welcome to go along with Lorelei, as long as your parents say it's okay."

I nod and shove another forkful of food into my mouth so I don't have to reply, and keep watching Lorelei's lips as she eats. I'm actually kind of jealous of the turkey for getting to be so close to her mouth.

After a moment, Lorelei yawns dramatically and puts her hand over her mouth. "I'm so tired from school, I think we will just go to bed early," Lorelei says. "You're tired too, right, Julie?" She's acting so cheerful I think her skin is turning a bit yellow, like her room has rubbed off on her.

I just nod and keep shovelling food. It's delicious. I don't want it to, but it keeps reminding me of my mom, so I both want to keep eating and push my plate away.

"Good . . . good," Pastor Greenwood says.

After dinner Lorelei excuses us both and we retreat to her room to get ready.

"They always go to bed really early on weekends because Dad has mass Saturday morning," she says, holding up a bright blue dress in front of herself in the mirror. I try not to think about Mom lying under a bedsheet all night while we sneak off to a party. I feel a bit guilty for not staying home when she's acting so weird. But how could I miss tonight? The soft memory of Lorelei's lips eases the guilt. I wouldn't have missed that for the world.

Sure enough, Lorelei's parents come by to say goodnight at 9:00 p.m. sharp. We're dressed in the disguise of our PJs while we bid them goodnight. After that we hear the click of their door and then Lorelei holds five fingers up in the air.

"Five minutes till Mother goes to the kitchen for a glass of water, then ten minutes till they're snoring," she says.

Fifteen minutes later we sneak to their bedroom door to make double sure. Sneaking around in Lorelei's house is a breeze, not like in mine where the neighbours across the street can hear when you're coming down the hall. We press our ears to the door, and beyond it I hear a tandem set of snores: one high, one low. Listening to that, I wonder if some people are just meant to be together. Do Lorelei and I snore in tandem when we have sleepovers?

Lorelei can't drive either so we have to walk for half an hour to get to the party. The city is strangely arranged; it can go from good to bad neighbourhoods in the span of a block or two. As we're walking a car slows down and some guy in the front seat whistles at us. It freaks me out a bit, but Lorelei seems to love it. She sticks out her chest and tosses her hair over her shoulder. The car crawls past and I'm afraid they're going to stop, but they just keep going. Then Lorelei looks at me and rolls her eyes, smiling like she gets that kind of reaction from people everywhere she goes.

"Boys," she says.

And I laugh awkwardly.

When we finally arrive I wobble on a pair of Lorelei's platform shoes up to the door of Jamal's house (we both changed out of our running shoes a block back). It's practically pulsing with loud music and bursting at the hinges with kids who are way older than us. This is not like any of the parties I've been to before, which mostly consist of presents and parents keeping an eye on us from a distance, or, once in a while, a dance in the school gym with a couple of depressed-looking streamers and watered-down punch. I guess I've had a pretty sheltered childhood. Lorelei looks one hundred percent more comfortable than me and is instantly absorbed into the crowd like she's been here the whole time. She's smiling and flirting while I weave and wobble behind her. I constantly tug my miniskirt, which is riding up near my butt, and try not to imagine Lorelei being completely absorbed by the crowd and leaving me alone.

"Isn't this great?" Lorelei asks, sliding up beside me as we make our way through the house.

"Yeah . . . ," I reply.

She laughs and grabs my hand and I hold on tight to her and feel her warmth seeping into me. Her confidence is reassuring. Maybe this *is* great. This is what teenage life is supposed to be like, right? Sneaking out, rowdy parties and short skirts. But the truth is I would rather be in her room, alone with her. Her body leaning into me. Her mouth on mine.

The grade-nine party is in the basement, so we make our way down. It's definitely tamer than what's going on upstairs—quieter and less packed. Half our grade is here, but I don't really know many of them. I do recognize some people though: Jamal, obviously, and Henry and also Josie and Carla and a couple of other people I share some classes with. Henry comes up to greet us and tries to hug Lorelei, but she just takes a step back and pushes me forward.

"Doesn't Julie look hot in this skirt?" she says.

Henry pauses and looks at me like he's at a gallery and I'm stuck on the wall. Then he gets this gleam in his eye. I'd like to say this is the point where I swoon and decide to focus all my romantic attention on Henry because he clearly likes the look of me, but that's not how feelings work. I will say, however, that it doesn't feel quite as gross as I thought it would to have someone other than Lorelei look at me with interest—even if it is a boy.

"Wanna drink?" Henry asks. He holds up a red

plastic cup and sloshes it around so the liquid splashes up the sides and spills over a little.

"I guess," I reply.

Lorelei's way ahead of us. She's already at the drinks table where there are a bunch of juice containers, a couple dozen skinny brown bottles of beer, some vodka and a half-full bottle of peppermint schnapps.

"Beer? This is amazing!" Lorelei says. She immediately grabs a bottle and cracks it open. She doesn't even bother using a cup.

"Yeah, I guess Jamal stole some from the party upstairs," Henry says.

Lorelei giggles and swigs from her bottle, then hands it over to me. I'm thrilled that my lips will touch the bottle where her lips just were. I take a tiny sip and gag. It's so bitter. I smile though, and nod like it's the most delicious thing I've ever tasted.

"You want your own?" she asks.

I shake my head and pour some fruit punch instead.

"Party pooper," Lorelei says, pouting at me a little.

I think about adding some vodka to my drink, but I really don't want to. No matter what Lorelei says.

The music upstairs pounds and thrums as we arrange ourselves in various groups and gossip. I mingle and make small talk with some of my classmates. After a while I abandon my platform shoes and sit down cross-legged on the floor beside Lorelei.

I keep a pillow on my lap though, because my skirt is so short. I lean on Lorelei, but try not to lean so hard that she decides she doesn't like it and wants me to move.

"Are you having fun?" Lorelei asks.

I nod and rest my head on her shoulder. She's almost done her second beer and takes a big swig to finish it off. "I'm glad you're here with me," she says.

"Me too." I close my eyes and feel her shoulder move up and down as she breathes and try not to think about the way my mom's breathing looked under the bedsheet, so slow and shallow. In and out.

"Rumour Has It!" Lorelei cries suddenly, and all the kids jump to attention. I take a deep breath and lift my head. Everyone both loves and hates this little party game. Rumour Has It is where you say all the rumours flying around the school at the moment and some people make up new ones. Everyone crowds around me and Lorelei in a tight little group. A bunch of people are sipping beers and makeshift cocktails. Suddenly we all look so young that I want to run home and crawl into the basket with JC and let my mom take care of me.

"Josie and Carla make out at sleepovers," Jamal says, starting the ball rolling with old news.

"Duh," Lorelei replies.

Josie and Carla grin, and with a decisiveness that

says *just for the record* turn to each other and lock lips. Everybody's mouths hang open as we watch. I feel a pang of jealousy in the lower part of my stomach—jealousy mixed with an electric buzz of excitement. I close my eyes for a second and imagine it's me and Lorelei kissing in the middle of the crowd. What would everyone think then? Would Lorelei want to make it public? When they finally pull away, all the boys applaud and whistle, except Henry and Jamal, who are probably just playing it cool.

After that the rumours just fly: there's one about a kid named Jack making out with his cousin, this guy Nicco smoking a whole pack of cigarettes at lunch, some girl named Hua shoplifting chocolate bars from the convenience store across from the school. Then Lorelei, eyes bright and looking right at me, says, "Henry's hot for Julie!"

Everyone goes "Ooooooh." Henry blushes and swirls his fruit punch. I narrow my eyes at Lorelei and consider saying, "Julie is in love with Lorelei," but there's no way I have the guts.

A bit of a silence follows and there are a few giggles. Then someone yells out, "Lorelei is having an affair with Mr. Gomez!" and everyone bursts into laughter except Lorelei, Henry and me. Lorelei's face is so still for a second it's creepy. Then she hiccups and starts laughing so hard it looks painful. I glance over at

Henry. We force a smile at each other and soon we're laughing along with everyone else.

After the game breaks up, Lorelei says she has to go to the washroom and runs upstairs. Henry slides down onto the floor to sit beside me, and I'm surprised that he doesn't smell like that crappy cologne. I guess he got the memo that it wasn't doing him any favours. I notice his shirt still looks a little dirty though, and I'm pretty sure it's the same one he was wearing the other night when we saw each other in the park, which is kind of nasty.

"I like your skirt," he says.

"It's not mine," I reply. I don't really feel like talking to him after Rumour Has It, and I'm considering running upstairs to find Lorelei. Obviously that stuff about her and Mr. Gomez is ridiculous, but her reaction wasn't what I expected.

Then Henry slips his hand onto my leg.

And it just feels clammy, not warm and amazing like Lorelei's. I look down at it, lying there limp on my leg, and I remember what Lorelei said about him liking it when girls take control. So instead of taking any control at all, I just stare at his hand until enough time passes that it's completely awkward. Then he moves it away and we both sit there in silence.

"Sorry," he says.

"It's okay," I reply. But it's really not okay.

"I just . . . " His voice trails off. This isn't the first time I've heard the great Henry Carter have nothing to say. What is his problem?

"What are you drinking?" I ask, trying to lighten the mood a little.

"Punch." He looks down at his cup and I notice that his teeth are red from the punch, and the stain has spread to his lips too, making them look lipstick-pink. It reminds me of Lorelei's lips, and I try not to stare.

"Oh," I reply.

"Yeah."

"Look, do you still like Lorelei?" I want to clear the air.

He snorts, but stays quiet. I don't know what that means. I steal a glance in his direction. His face looks both relaxed and tense at the same time, if that's possible.

"Sometimes things make no sense, Julie," Henry says. The way the words come out sound like a balloon deflating. His shoulders follow suit and he sinks into the carpet. I don't know what to say. I think about my mom in the parlour, buried beneath the Egyptian cotton bedsheet, and I couldn't agree more, but I certainly don't want the most meaningful moment of my night to be my agreement with Henry Carter.

So I just ask, "What do you mean?"

His eyes search my face like he's looking for something he lost. "It's just, people aren't always what they seem, you know?"

I think about Lorelei, somewhere upstairs in the bathroom, maybe texting on her secret cellphone. She's been gone for too long now and I'm starting to get antsy. This isn't the first time she's ditched me, or disappeared when I need her. She does this a lot more than I even want to admit.

"I know," I reply.

"Like you," he says.

That surprises me. "Me?"

"I thought you hated me," he says, "that you would never talk to me."

"I don't hate you, Henry, it's just . . . complicated."

He laughs. "You always glare at me, and your face gets all grossed out when I'm around."

The truth is I didn't think he ever noticed me, because he's always completely preoccupied with Lorelei. It's weird to think that, all this time, he has. I feel guilty, caught in the act.

"Sorry, I just . . . you know, you're not so bad."

"Neither are you," he says.

We both laugh this time. Then Henry looks off into the distance, beyond the party, maybe even beyond this moment. Sometimes people aren't what they seem and sometimes they don't want to show it. So I don't try to force conversation. I just slide a micrometre closer to Henry so he can feel me beside him. Something tells me he doesn't want to feel alone right now.

I'm not really sure how long we stay in the basement, or how long Lorelei is gone, because I can't see a clock. It feels like forever though. When she finally comes back down, her hair is arranged differently and her cheeks are bright red. I force myself not to ask where she was. She looks beautiful, and all I want to do is grab her and hold her tight.

She smiles and holds out her hand. "It's time to go home," she says.

5.

I got a bad flu when I was five. I was sick for days and my mom moved into my room. She slept on the floor beside me, and when I was tossing and turning at night she would crawl into bed with me and wrap me up tight in her arms. It was the first time I remember consciously thinking that she and I were different people. Her heart was beating slower than mine; her breathing was so quiet. Then I put my arms around her too. Even though I was the one who was sick, I thought maybe she was the one who needed a hug.

Lorelei and I are lying side by side in bed, which, of course, is totally normal. But now I'm hoping we'll kiss again, maybe even get to second base. It's dark in the room but I can see the whites of Lorelei's eyes and feel the glow of the yellow walls. And all of a sudden I'm super fond of the walls. I think if I asked really nicely I could convince my parents to let me paint my walls yellow in homage. It probably wouldn't even be that hard to get my mom to say yes in her current state.

"Did you kiss him?" Lorelei asks, finally breaking the silence.

"No," I say. "He put his hand on my leg."

She snorts a laugh that lacks her usual Lorelei lyricism. "How risqué."

"Where did you go?" I ask. I can't hold it in any longer.

I can feel her whole body shrug; it moves the covers. "Just upstairs. I had to find the bathroom; there was a line."

I don't believe her, but I would never say so.

"He likes you, you know," she says, her voice dropping to a conspiratorial whisper. "I thought so before, but I could definitely tell when he saw you in that skirt."

"He likes *you*," I say. "He was just distracted by the skirt, or maybe he thought I looked like you in it."

"No way. I know Henry and he's totally smitten with you." She's moving closer now that she's feeling insistent. I can feel her breath on my face and it smells a bit peachy. I try to remember if there was peach juice at the party. "Trust me," she whispers.

But I'm not sure that I do. It's weird how you can want someone so badly but still not trust them.

"I think I was just freaked out. I'm still not sure I'm good at kissing." I lie to her face.

"You're fine," she says. "You're good, actually, better than a lot of people I've kissed, but I guess I've never kissed another girl before, so it's hard to compare."

A small thrill vibrates in my chest. She thinks I'm a good kisser. "What other guys have you kissed?" I ask.

Another full body shrug. "Dunno, a bunch, whatever." Her *whatever* is not the kind of *whatever* that equals not caring though. It's the kind of *whatever* that someone says when they don't want to keep talking about something because they're embarrassed. How many guys *has* she kissed?

"Maybe I need some more practice," I say. No, I squeak it. The words that come out of my mouth are barely words, they're so high-pitched and breathy.

Lorelei laughs and puts her hand on my shoulder. But she doesn't move in to kiss me; she just stays super still and breathes steadily. I close my eyes and listen.

After a while I think of Henry, deflated in the basement beside me.

"When you were with Henry, did he ever seem, I dunno, sad?" I ask.

Lorelei slides her hand off my shoulder. "No. What do you mean? He's just Henry. He's not that deep." She laughs a little.

"Do you think you need to be deep to be sad?" I ask.

"I guess not. I don't know. I was just joking. I

guess sometimes Henry got a bit down when we were together, but who doesn't, Julie? We all have our moments, right?"

"Did you ever talk to him about it?"

"We didn't really talk that much," she says. She shifts around and I can see little wisps of her hair, wayward in the shadows. "God, I guess that makes me shallow."

Her voice has an unfamiliar tone of doubt. "No!" I say, quickly. "No, it doesn't. Maybe you two just didn't have anything in common. Not like us. Right?" I try to think of all the things Lorelei and I have in common, but I can't pinpoint anything specific.

"Maybe," she says, her voice dropping low.

I reach out and put my hand on her shoulder. "Definitely." Even if she is a little shallow, so what? I'm not the deepest person in the world either—who is?

"It was just that Henry seemed a bit sad tonight, that's all," I say. "It's no big deal; it's just Henry."

"Well, you can ask him when you're his girlfriend then." The old Lorelei is back. She pinches my arm and I roll onto my back, laughing.

"I'm not going to be his girlfriend," I say. *I want to be yours.*

"Whatever. Goodnight, dahling, I'm exhausted," she says. Then she rolls over and everything is quiet except for my beating heart and Lorelei's quiet exhalations in the dark.

I'm not sure if I even sleep at all; it's hard to say. I'm too busy listening to Lorelei breathe and hoping she'll roll over and grab onto me. But come morning I'm up and eating breakfast with the Greenwoods. Everyone is smiling at each other with their straight white teeth. There are perfect piles of pancakes on our plates, with these perfect little squares of butter on them. We chat a bit about nothing in particular and I help clear up the dishes when we're done. After that I say thank you to Pastor and Mrs. Greenwood and hug Lorelei goodbye. I wish I could kiss her goodbye too, but I'm too much of a wuss for that, obviously.

When I get home Dad and JC are in the living room watching TV. Although I guess it would be more accurate to say Dad is watching TV and JC is watching Dad. It's a rare sight, seeing Dad doing anything except working and eating.

"Where's Mom?" I ask.

"Hello to you too," Dad says without taking his eyes off the TV. He's watching some sort of science documentary. I can tell because I recognize the Large Hadron Collider from a project I did when they first turned it on.

"Sorry, hi," I say. "Where's Mom?"

"She's at Anna's."

Anna of the sage and crystals, of the massaging hands that are somehow supposed to cure Mom of her missing heart.

The TV says the Large Hadron Collider has completely proven the existence of the Higgs boson. This should be distractingly interesting, but I have other things on my mind. The warm softness of the kiss with Lorelei. Henry's hand on my leg. Whether Anna's magic hands were able to massage the weirdness right out of Mom.

Dad and I watch TV for at least two hours, and Dad says it's okay because it's educational. I'm not sure Mom would see it that way though, if she were in a state of mind to see anything in any way. Eventually we hear the car pull into the driveway and Mom comes in. JC does a chirp like a little bird because he seems to know it's her even if he can't see her.

"How was your massage?" I ask. I turn around on the couch to look at her. I'm sad to report she doesn't look any different, like not at all, which makes me even more skeptical of stupid Anna and her stupid crystal healing powers.

"Yeah," Mom replies, as if that's an actual answer to my question.

"Come watch this special on cryptids, honey,"

Dad says. A picture of the Loch Ness monster flashes across the screen, and at this point I'm pretty sure we've passed out of the realm of educational viewing. I turn again to look at Mom. For once in my life I hope she'll tell us to turn off the TV because it'll rot our brains. But instead she just creaks up the stairs, down the hall and into the bedroom, after which I hear the distant flop of her falling onto the bed.

"She's just tired—a massage takes a lot out of you. Actually, they recommend you take a nap afterwards," Dad says. Then he cranks up the volume on the cryptid show and we watch a bunch of guys in army fatigues talk about their techniques for hunting Big Foot.

It's just me and Dad at dinner because Mom's still asleep. So we order pizza and keep watching TV. Eventually it gets so dark in the room that the only light is a slice of brightness from the screen.

"I'm worried about Mom," I say during a commercial for Mini-Wheats. The Mini-Wheats are all smiling and dancing and being sugared in some factory. It makes it seem cruel that they end up in a bowl and we eat them. I guess that's how vegetarians feel.

"Don't worry, she's tough. She just needs extra rest right now because of JC. Being a mom is tiring. Just remember that when the boys come a-knocking."

I think about Henry, deflated on the floor beside me at the party. "You have nothing to worry about there.

But seriously, Mom is . . . " I'm really considering telling him about everything—her missing heart, her bedsheet antics—but I can't do that to Mom. I promised I would keep her secret and, no matter how heavy it weighs, I want to keep my promise. "She's acting weird."

Dad laughs, but I'm not sure if he's laughing at me or Bart Simpson. We definitely left educational TV behind about three hours ago, and now I'm positive we're just rotting our brains.

"Don't worry," Dad says. He reaches over absently and puts his hand on my shoulder. He's so tired and spaced out I'm pretty sure he's not even really listening to me.

I smile at him, then retire to my room.

Once again I'm jarred awake by JC. I sneak over to my door and stick my head out. The crying isn't coming from downstairs, so I know Mom will be up soon and at JC's side. I wait a bit until I see her, silver and silent in the hallway, cradling the baby. I step out into the hall. *Creeaaaakkk.* Mom turns to look at me.

"Are you going out driving?" I ask.

"Yes," she whispers.

"Wait for me."

I run back into my room and slip into my red-paint hoodie and a pair of jeans. This time I'm not letting

94

her go alone. This time I'm not waiting in the street, worrying that she's zoned out behind the wheel. Fully dressed, I race back out to the hall. Mom has already gone downstairs, so I run after her and make it to the car just as she's tucking my screeching brother into the baby seat in the back. I slip into the front and do up my seatbelt. Then Mom gets in and starts the car.

"This is so cool," I say unconvincingly as the neighbourhood passes by outside the window. "Are you feeling better?" I look over at Mom but she's looking straight ahead and her fingers are clamped around the steering wheel in a way that suddenly makes me wonder if she's actually awake.

"Mom?" I reach out and squeeze her shoulder and she tenses a little.

"Yeah," she says. But I'm not sure if she's saying yeah she's feeling better or if she was just responding to me saying "Mom."

"Sometimes I wish we could just drive forever." I'm really only saying that for something to say. If we drove forever I would never get to see Lorelei again, never get to feel those soft lips. The kiss replays in my mind for like the millionth time and I can't help but smile.

"Yeah," Mom says again.

We ride in silence for a bit. JC has calmed down in the back, so much so that when I turn to look he's actually asleep. I lean my forehead against the window and look out. The city looks amazing beneath the big silver moon, kind of like a black-and-white movie. I would like to think maybe this is my version of clandestine womanly bonding times.

"Do you like old movies?" I ask.

Mom just shrugs, so I shrug back and keep quiet. It's not long though until I start to feel that there's something familiar about the route. We pass through Regent Park and then take a right onto the highway, then another right up along Pottery Road. Now I know where we're going, because Mom makes us go here every two weeks with colourful bouquets of wildflowers, bundled together in bursts of magenta and lilac, crimson and peach.

"Why are we going to the graveyard?" I ask. All the sleepiness drains out of me and my limbs feel electrified. I look over at Mom and she's still really pale, ghostly in the streetlight. "Mom, seriously, like I get it every two weeks for Grandpa James, but at midnight? With JC?" If I'm starting to lose my cool a bit it's because a graveyard at midnight seems almost like inviting supernatural trouble. It's not that I actually believe in ghosts, but better safe than sorry, right?

"It's okay," Mom says flatly. As if that makes it all better.

I look back at JC. He's totally unconcerned, his

face arranged into this sleepy, pudgy sculpture that would be pretty adorable if it wasn't such a betrayal. Why should he get to be so relaxed when I'm forced to deal with Mom?

We turn left into Mount Pleasant Cemetery and take these small, windy roads all the way to the section with Grandpa James's grave. Then Mom parks and we sit there for a bit in the ticking car as the moon shines down on the rows of graves jutting out from the earth like dirty old crooked teeth. Mom looks out the window toward Grandpa James's grave. Her hands are clenched tight on the steering wheel. Her fingers look so thin I'm pretty sure that at any moment one of her bones is going to pierce through, then the rest of her skin will slough off and all she'll be is a skeleton.

"Now what?" I say.

But she doesn't respond; she just opens the door and slips away into the dark. At this point I'm torn between staying with JC and chasing after Mom to make sure she doesn't do something crazy like dig up Grandpa James's body. Last summer someone went shopping at the Sherway Gardens mall for like five hours and left their baby in the car. People had to smash the windows to get the kid out, but he died of heat stroke. He was around JC's age, so needless to say I'm not excited at the prospect of leaving him alone. But then again, it's only spring. I unbuckle and hop out of the car and chase Mom down the nearest line of graves toward Grandpa James's.

I don't like the fact that you have to walk on other people's graves to get to the one you want to visit—it feels disrespectful. Plus, I've seen those movies with dead hands shooting up from the ground. So I tiptoe over the graves of Martha Murray, Sal Halcone, Camden Parsons, Nicolas Price, Francine Hamilton and so forth. I say sorry under my breath as I go, just in case there's something going on down there, afterlife-wise.

Mom is looking down at Grandpa James's grave.

"We can't just leave JC in the car, you know," I say.

"Let's play a game," she replies.

"What do you mean, play a game? It's late and JC is in the car. Is this what you do with him when you drive around at night, Mom?" All the parts of my body are tense: my back, my shoulders, my neck. I feel the almost-painful throbbing of my heart in my throat. I'm near panic now, in this quiet, ghoulish graveyard in the middle of the night.

"It's called Rest in Peace," she continues, "where you say all the nice things you can think about me, just like we did for Grandpa James when he died."

"This is insane," I say. "You're not dead. Grandpa James is, but you're not. Plus, you can't leave JC alone. He's a baby, and babies can't survive without us. Mom? Seriously!"

And I was worried she would zone out and crash the car. Somehow this feels a million times worse. What is this awful game she wants to play? She's hunched in the moonlight, a thin, shadowy line against the backdrop of the cemetery. I'm trying to breathe properly but my breath is only coming in short, quick bursts.

"Mom. Seriously, let's go. Mommy?" I haven't called her *Mommy* since I was little. It feels so immature, but that's exactly what I am right now. I want to have a temper tantrum, to scream and kick like a little kid who didn't get to go to the zoo. Anything to make Mom remember that I'm supposed to be the kid and she's supposed to be the adult. The mature one.

But she doesn't respond. She just keeps staring at Grandpa James's grave, her face drawn into a slight frown. I don't know what to do. I reach out and touch her arm but she doesn't respond. Her skin is cold to the touch.

"Okay, Mom. Do you promise to go if I play the game?"

"Yes."

"Okay. Fine. Well, you're beautiful . . . ," I start.

"No," she says, quietly insistent, "you have to say it past tense. I *was* beautiful . . . " She doesn't look at me when she talks, and I hate that I can't see into her eyes. I feel a pressure in my chest, like a big hand is opening in my solar plexus.

Past tense. *Was, were, used to be.*

"I don't want to play this game. This sucks," I say. "I want to go." A cool breeze picks up and runs its icy fingers through my hair, making me shiver.

"Just a bit," she says, her voice a little desperate. "Just for a minute." She still doesn't look at me, she's staring so intently at Grandpa James's grave.

"Okay fine, one minute." I take a deep breath and close my eyes, trying to think of something, anything to say. "Mom is . . . *was* beautiful and she *made* good macaroni and she *was* an amazing, heroic firefighter before she had JC. She *was* a wonderful mom who always listened and helped me with my homework and took care of me when I was sick." I'm saying all the things that pop into my mind about Mom, but when they're stacked up, one after another, it all seems painfully shallow. This is the woman who gave birth to me, raised me, loved me, and all I can say about her is that she made good macaroni? I don't know if my pathetic list says more about her or me.

I open my eyes and there's Mom, just nodding in the dark.

And I want to keep going but my mind is blank.

Why can't I think of more things to say about her?

Tears creep up behind my eyes and threaten to spill over. The cemetery is silent but for the wind and the quiet sound of our breath, and I don't know what else to say. So all I say is "Game over," and then I grab her cold, cold hand and pull her back across all those creepy graves, all the way to the car, where JC is still waiting, sleeping soundly like we never left at all.

6.

When I was six my hamster, Harry, died. I didn't know what that meant, and Mom had to tell me. She didn't try to sugar-coat it or anything. She just said, "Harry stopped breathing. His brain shut down. He stopped being Harry." I didn't cry when she said that, even though she told me it was okay if I wanted to. We made a tiny coffin for him and buried him in the backyard. Mom and Dad looked sad, and Mom told me to say a few words, but I couldn't think of anything because all I felt was an empty space where Harry once was. So I didn't say anything, I just cried instead. And Mom held my hand and stayed quiet.

Mom stays in her room all day the next day. Dad feeds me and JC and takes a tray up to Mom for lunch. It's strange to see him doing household stuff like making food, because usually my mom does that. He tells me Mom's just not feeling well—I guess she's tired from our late-night graveyard visit.

The thought of it sends shivers racing across my skin. I hated that stupid game and I never want to play it again.

I call Lorelei in the afternoon. She sounds happy to hear from me, but not even close to how happy I am to be talking to her.

"I was zonked all day yesterday," she says, "but Father made me go to church today to hear his sermon about loving your neighbour or whatever. It was so boring."

I lie back in my bed and imagine Lorelei is right beside me.

"Anyway, Henry texted and he was asking all these questions about you—what you're like and if you're cool and stuff." She pauses for effect, like I should be super appreciative and falling all over myself to find out what he thinks of me. But I can't get last night out of my head. The quiet in the graveyard. My horribly shallow eulogy.

"Have you ever heard of a living person acting dead?" I ask, trying to sound as casual as possible.

There's a long silence and I hear a shifting sound on the other end of the line.

"What?" Lorelei says.

"I don't mean zombies . . . I mean . . . I don't know, people, like, pretending they're dead?"

"That's weird, Julie, and what are you talking about? Did you hear what I said about Henry?"

"Yeah, it's just that I'm writing a story so I wanted to know if you've ever heard of anything like that."

"No." She sounds terse and kind of bored.

"Sorry," I say. But the apology falls flat because I don't really mean it. We're supposed to be able to talk about everything because we're best friends, but it always seems like we only discuss what *she* wants to talk about.

"It's okay. Anyway, so I told Henry you were totally cool, of course, and he should ask you out. Then he said he might want to ask you to the Spring Fling, so I absolutely told him yes."

"Oh." I guess I won't be able to talk to Lorelei about my mom.

"Listen, I know you're weirded out about the whole kissing thing, but I promise you'll be fine with Henry," Lorelei says. "If I liked kissing you, he will too."

My whole body tingles when she says that last bit.

"Really?" I ask. What I meant to ask was if she really liked kissing me, but it came out as nervousness about Henry instead.

"Of course!" she says, before I can correct myself. "So, you'll go to the dance with him?"

"I don't know," I say. I'm stuck; I can't fix my stupid mistake now. I can't do anything now short of admitting how I feel about her, and I'm too much of a coward for that. "When you broke up with him, you said he was kind of lame."

"I was just mad. But I'm so over it, and I think you guys would be totally cute together. You have to at least kiss one guy before grade ten, Julie. I'm pretty sure it's mandatory."

I laugh. "That's ludicrous." *I kissed you. That counts, doesn't it?*

"It's true," she says, giggling.

"But we were supposed to go to the dance together . . . alone," I say.

"That was before the Henry thing."

"Why do you want me to do this so badly?"

"I love love, dahling," she says. I can practically feel her flipping her hair through the phone.

"Okay, fine," I say. I want to kick myself for being such a wimp.

She claps and squeals so loud I have to move the phone away from my ear. I knew I wasn't actually going to the dance *with* her, but we were still planning to go together. And now I'm stuck with Henry. I mean, it's not that Henry's so bad, I guess, it's just he's not my date of choice, obviously.

"Oh, this is perfect," she says. "You guys are going to be so hot."

Hot is Lorelei kneeling next to me and putting her lips on mine. Hot is not Henry's limp hand on my thigh in a half-hearted attempt at seduction.

"How's the poster coming, by the way?" she asks.

"I'll have something for you by Thursday," I reply.

I'm going to have to work on it tonight if I want to get it done.

"Purrrfect," she says. But I don't laugh.

After I hang up I google "pretending you're dead," but all I get is 21,100,000 hits for people playing dead during attacks. Frustrated for obvious reasons, I get to work on the poster and come up with a halfway decent design before I decide to call it quits. I crawl into bed early because I got practically zero hours of sleep last night and I have to be a normal school-attending person tomorrow. I lie awake for another hour at least.

Dad's already left for work when I get up the next morning, and Mom is still in her room. Dad left a packed lunch though, and some money so I could eat breakfast at Starbucks. I can't hear JC, so that must mean he's with Mom in my parents' room. I wonder if the fact that the whole house feels so tense will cause him some sort of trauma when he's older. I've heard that kind of thing really affects babies.

The air is fresh outside, not like the stale air in the house. Every part of me feels elated to be away from home, drinking coffee at Starbucks and going to school like a normal person.

When I approach the school, Henry appears. He's like one big, tight smile. He grabs my elbow and escorts me in as if we're in a world where men still escort women places. Someone whistles at us in the hall by my locker; it's insanely embarrassing. I rip my arm away from him and his smile falters. I feel bad for him for just a second.

"I have to go to class," I say.

He stands with his arms at his sides and he suddenly looks so meek, like he was at the party. This different side of Henry still surprises me. Just a couple of days ago in the schoolyard he looked so intense and collected, kicking that ball around with his soccer legs and eyeing Lorelei like she was the only girl for a thousand miles. Now his eyes look dim and faraway. I try not to think of Mom and her hollow gaze. *Mom* was *a wonderful person.*

"Okay. Um, do you want to have lunch together?" he asks.

I shrug. "I guess, but I'm probably eating with Lorelei."

"That's cool."

We stand facing each other and it seems like neither of us knows what to say. Luckily the bell knows exactly what to say, and it rings loudly through the halls. We both startle and run off to our respective classes.

This morning it's history.

"Today we're moving on to a new unit," Mr. Gomez

says. "Ancient Greece. We're going to discuss the Greek pantheon and some ancient philosophers."

At this point, the door opens and Lorelei comes rushing in, cheeks stained with hurry.

"Sorry," she says, "our power went out and . . . "

"Please take a seat, Miss Greenwood," Mr. Gomez says, voice stern.

Lorelei dips her head in a little bow and scampers up the row to her seat. She stares at me with wide eyes, then winks. My stomach contracts with happiness. Maybe I shouldn't have chickened out of telling her about my feelings. Maybe I should just do it at lunch and get it over with. The very thought of it sends me reeling, excitement and stress mixing together in a big tight knot in my chest.

"Back to Greece," Mr. Gomez says. "Please open your textbooks to page one forty-three."

Lorelei and I finally get a chance to talk as the rest of the class filters out of the room after class.

"I saw Henry in the hall and we got to talking about you, so of course I was late," she whispers, taking my hand and pulling me toward the door of the classroom.

"Miss Greenwood?" It's Mr. Gomez.

Lorelei whips around when she hears her name.

"Yes, Mr. Gomez?" she says, her voice unnaturally high and sweet.

"I'll need to see you in this classroom at lunch to talk about your late arrival." He's wiping the chalk off the board. It's all over his hands and there's even some in his hair.

"Okay," Lorelei replies. Then she turns back toward me and rolls her eyes. We run off to the bathroom together while everyone chats in the halls.

"So, Henry says he wants to eat lunch with you." Lorelei is at the mirror applying her lipstick. I'm lounging against the wall, trying to think of a way out of my lunch date. If I'm going to confess everything to Lorelei, we need to be alone together.

"Yeah, but I said I eat lunch with you," I reply.

"Oh, but this is perfect then, because Mr. Gomez will probably keep me in all lunch."

"Why would he keep you if you tell him your power failed and your alarm didn't go off?"

"Oh, you know him. He loves doling out the punishments," she says. She caps her lipstick and makes a kissy face in the mirror before adjusting her boobs.

"How do I look?" she asks.

Perfect. "Fine," I say.

"Just fine?" she pouts.

"Great."

She beams and turns to me. My heart stops beating for a few seconds.

"Well, anyway, Henry's going to ask you to the dance at lunch, just so you're not surprised."

I roll my eyes and she laughs. Then she steps forward and sweeps me into an awkward slow-dance pose: her hands on my hips, mine resting lightly on her shoulders. We sway a little and I laugh. Our faces are so close I could just lean over and kiss her again. Right now.

"You don't have to pretend; I get that you're excited," she says.

"It's not that, it's just . . . "

She crinkles her brow so dramatically with concern that it looks like a caricature. "What?" she says.

I'm trying to get my lips to form the words, but I can't. Then, of course, the door swings open and Josie and Carla walk in hand in hand, giggling. They stop when they see us.

"Sorry! Are we interrupting something?" Josie asks, eyes sparkling beneath her thick, stylish fringe that falls just above her eyebrows.

Lorelei grins. "Of course not, ladies. And I fully expect to see you at the meeting on Wednesday, with updates for me."

Both Josie and Carla give weak smiles and army salutes. And we all stand and watch as Lorelei nods, then turns and sashays out the door, leaving me alone with Josie and Carla.

"So, are you two going to go at it already, or what?"

Josie asks, leaning against the wall in a more relaxed fashion than I could ever master. My heart constricts to the size of a pea. Carla watches me with narrowed eyes and I feel stuck, glued in place.

"I . . . ," I whisper.

"It's just so obvious—you're totally heart-eyed around her," Josie continues. "I think she would go for it too, even though she's a bit of a homophobe."

I don't know what to do with this information. My heart is thunking hard and my face feels like it's been painted bright red.

"Well, how did you . . . ?" I manage to squeak in the general direction of the girls.

Josie beams and reaches out for Carla's hand. She looks so comfortable slipping her fingers into Carla's that a thrill of jealousy races up my arms.

"One night when she was sleeping over, I just slid my arm around her waist and I felt her heart kick into high gear. She turned around and melted into me."

"It was perfect," Carla murmurs, proving, once and for all, that she can actually speak.

"I couldn't do that," I say, thinking of all the opportunities that have passed me by. "I'm too much of a coward." I close my eyes for a second and picture my kiss with Lorelei, the briefest moment in her sunlit yellow bedroom. Could I have taken it further? Could I have asked for more?

I shake my head and Josie laughs.

"Well, whatever. You should just go for it. YOLO, right?"

Carla snorts a tiny laugh and I try to smile.

"Maybe," I say.

Josie shrugs and pulls on Carla's hand. Then the two of them vanish into the wheelchair stall together. I'm literally burning with envy as I hear them laughing behind the closed door.

"Good luck," Josie says, her voice echoing off the tiles and hitting me hard.

When the lunch bells rings, I'm forced out into the hall to find Henry after waving goodbye to Lorelei, who is heading over to Mr. Gomez's classroom. I still feel pretty sad for Mr. Gomez, because Ayesha Hai told me the other day that she heard he walks his cat—*actually walks his cat*, with a leash and everything. How pathetic is that? Maybe I'll still be able to muster the courage to tell Lorelei everything at lunch, as long as Mr. Gomez doesn't keep her too long. Unfortunately, I don't have to look far for Henry, because he's right outside my class.

"I thought we could eat in the yard," he says.

"Sure," I reply.

We walk outside.

"Where's your lunch?" Henry asks when we're standing beside the picnic table.

"Oh, crap," I say, racing through my day to remember where I left it. "I think I forgot it in my first period class. Duh."

He laughs. "Do you want me to go grab it?"

"No. Just stay here. I'll be back." I take off at a run, through the yard, through the empty halls and onward to Mr. Gomez's classroom.

Now here I am pushing open the door and looking around for my lunch. And here's Mr. Gomez sitting on top of his desk. With Lorelei right beside him. Their thighs pressed together. His eagle nose pointing down and her bright red lips pointing up. Looking like they are at that moment right before a kiss when the air is tight and anything is possible.

Here I am, eyes wide, collapsing in on myself, the centre of my own gravity pulling me down and in and down and in. Everything looks flat now, just lines and shapes floating across my vision. And here is Lorelei, hair flipping in Mr. Gomez's face as she turns and slides off the desk. She hits the ground, stepping toward me, mouth formed into the shape of a word that I don't want to hear.

My vision is all black, then full colour, black, then full colour—all the colours of Lorelei bent in all the angles of her.

She's taking another step toward me, saying more words I can't hear—we are all in slow motion. Mr. Gomez looks surprised and Lorelei looks pleading and I'm sure I look like nothing at all because I'm no longer here. I'm just a single dot of me where all my lines and angles used to be.

"I'm sick" is all I can muster before I turn and run, run, run all the way home.

7.

I broke my arm when I was seven. I tried to jump off a swing in the park and landed all wrong. Mom laughed at first when I wiped out, then her whole face fell and she rushed over. My dad was away on business so my mom had to call 911. We rode in an ambulance and it was actually pretty exciting. Mom said sorry like a million times and I told her it was okay. She said, "It's not okay! I can't believe I laughed." I said, "It was funny though." She just shook her head. It's the first time I can ever remember trying to comfort her. I had always thought parents didn't need us to make them feel better. I always thought it was just us who needed them.

It's the middle of the day when I run through the front door of my house. The air is so thick inside it's almost grey.

Now what?

Mom is finally out of her room. She's sitting at the dining-room table and she's still looking worn and pale. JC is in his basket gurgling and chewing on something that looks like a toy donkey. I walk over and sit across from Mom at the table. She's looking down at her hands.

"What are you thinking about?" I ask. I'm breathless but she doesn't notice. I shouldn't even be home right now, but she doesn't notice that either.

"Nothing," she replies.

Somehow this doesn't surprise me, not even a little. Of course she's thinking about nothing. Alone here in the dining room in the thick grey air of this creaky old house. What else could she be thinking about?

I focus for a minute on pushing Lorelei and Mr. Gomez out of my mind. His gold-rimmed eyes and eagle nose poised to touch the face of God within Lorelei. Did I really see that? It seems impossible. I was so ready to tell Lorelei everything, and then—that.

Suddenly, an image of Henry pops into my mind. Sitting alone and waiting in the yard. I completely forgot about him. I'm not even sure I have room in my brain to feel bad.

"Fine. Perfect. Sounds relaxing to think about nothing. I think I'll try it too," I say. "Because I could really use some not thinking about anything right about now." I fold my hands on the table and lean forward. She looks at me for another minute then just shrugs a bit, as if she's given in to my challenge without a fight. It's totally unrewarding, but again, not surprising.

The phone rings.

Brrrrrring. Brrrrrring. Brrrrrring.

The sound of it fills the whole house. JC makes tiny whining noises from his basket, but Mom doesn't make a move to pick up the phone. Neither do I. I know it's Lorelei, calling on her secret cellphone. She's already been calling and texting my cell non-stop, but I guess she wanted to try a new tactic. I know she'll probably say nothing happened; they were just talking and I'm blowing things out of proportion. But I saw what I saw. Didn't I? They almost kissed. And it makes sense too. Why wouldn't Mr. Gomez want to kiss Lorelei? I want to kiss her. Half the school wants to kiss her. Plus, she's always saying she likes mature men. I just—stupidly—didn't get the hint.

Brrrrrring. Brrrrrring. Brrrrrring.

"Can we go out, Mom?" I ask. "Can we just go somewhere? Anywhere?"

Mom nods, gets up and walks to the front door. She grabs her keys while I grab JC.

I'm happy to be on the road and I roll the window down. Feeling the wind on my face and the motion of the car eases the thought of Lorelei and Mr. Gomez, so at least that's something. And this time, we're not heading to the graveyard. Instead, we drive east into the burbs of Scarborough. Everything gets wide and all the buildings are low-slung, like little shoeboxes with driveways.

After a long, quiet ride we pull into a big, mostly empty parking lot. It leads to a building with a sign that says Casket Depot in big ornate cursive letters. As if the word *depot* could somehow not be tacky. My stomach drops to the floor and I feel a weight pressing on my temples, giving me a headache.

"What are we doing here, Mom?" I ask.

"I just want to look," Mom replies.

"Why?"

"I'm just looking," she whispers.

We get out and Mom starts walking so I grab JC. He's still chewing on the thing that looks like a donkey, only now he's chewing on a spot where the donkey has a squeaky bit, so it's making a high-pitched hee-haw. I wonder for a second if it's a dog toy. When we enter the Casket Depot it smells of metal and wood and maybe something like shoe polish. I'm pretty much immediately overwhelmed by the high ceilings and walls full of coffins. Mom, of course, looks completely unfazed by the whole situation. She steps forward into the huge warehouse and starts touching each casket as if they are all holy relics.

At this point, a short, plump, sweet-faced woman appears. She's wearing various shades of purple, which strikes me as odd—you'd think she would be wearing black, given the context. Maybe she's just trying to bring a little joy to the whole crappy idea of coffin shopping.

"Good afternoon, dear," she says. She instantly reminds me of this substitute teacher I had in grade six who called everyone dearie and brought in lollipops to reward us with. So for that week, everyone was acting really good so they would get a lollipop. She gave out so many that parents started to complain because their kids were coming home with stomachaches.

"Hi," I say. I bob JC up and down in my arms while he squeaks away at his donkey chew-toy: *hee-haw, hee-haw.*

"And what is this charming little gentleman's name?" the woman asks.

"JC," I reply. I'm pretty sure the woman's eyes are violet too. I wonder if she's wearing contacts, or if it's just the colour from her sweater reflecting onto her irises. "JC stands for James Christopher, our grandpas' names."

She beams. "That's lovely. May I?" But she reaches out before I have the chance to say she may, and she does this really babyish coochy-coo thing to JC's belly. He stops chewing his donkey for a second to stare at her like it's the strangest thing that's ever happened to him.

"Adorable," she says.

Meanwhile, Mom is somewhere in the back of the warehouse, probably still touching all the coffins.

"I'm Julie," I say.

"Hi, Julie. I'm Violet."

It's all I can do not to say something completely sarcastic at this point.

"How...thematic!" I reply, trying to sound bright.

"How can I help you today, Julie?"

"Well, I guess we've come for a coffin," I say. I can't believe I'm talking about this like it's some normal thing mothers and daughters do for fun.

"Oh dear, I'm so sorry," she replies. As though it's only now she's realized that the reason we're here — at the Casket Depot — is indeed for a coffin, and that means someone must have died. "And who is it that you've lost?" she asks. Her face is doing this thing where it's not just her lips that are pouting but all of her: her cheeks, her eyes, her chin. It seems like an almost impossible expression, but she's actually pulling it off.

"Well, it's for my mom, I guess." Because that's what we've been building to, haven't we? *I can't feel my heartbeat. Let's play a game. Mom used to make good macaroni.* My temples pulse as my pressure headache builds. Mom appears as if on cue from behind a big white gleaming coffin. Violet looks over at her, then back at me, then back at my mom, then down at JC.

"Oh, I'm so sorry," she says.

"Yeah," I reply. I'm not sure what else to say, so I just sort of walk away and start touching caskets myself to see if I can feel what Mom is feeling in them—if she's feeling anything at all. This place is so big it reminds me of a church. But the Casket Depot is made of steel, not wood, and the sun is shining though clear windows instead of stained glass. Even so, it feels holy, and now I'm wondering what actually makes a place holy—is it the name? The atmosphere? Or is it just because someone holy plunks themselves down in it and claims it as a holy spot?

We're surrounded by caskets, and it's so quiet it's actually kind of nice—peaceful even. I see a smaller coffin tucked away in the corner on the ground. It's dark brown like the colour of earth and I think it's just about the perfect size for me. So I walk over and touch it. I can see my reflection in the shellac.

"Julie?" Violet's reflection appears behind mine. "Are you okay over here?"

Of course I'm not okay. My mom is forcing me to coffin shop and images of Lorelei and Mr. Gomez together on the desk are practically burned into my eyelids, so I see them every time I blink.

"I don't know," I reply.

"Come on now, sweetheart," she says. She sounds reluctant. She reaches out her hand and I take it. It's so much warmer than my mom's hand that it makes me sad.

"This is really no place for a baby," Violet says, looking down at JC.

"Unless the baby's dead."

Violet frowns. "Yes, I suppose unless the baby is dead," she says.

Then she sweeps me along through the Casket Cathedral—a name I just invented for this place because it reminds me of a cathedral and it sounds way nicer than "depot"—toward the front where Mom isn't waiting because Mom isn't there at all.

"Mrs. . . . um . . . ," Violet stammers.

"Olive, her name is Olive," I say.

"Olive?"

Nothing. No Mom. I roll my eyes and JC squeaks and giggles. We go coffin to coffin looking for her.

She's chosen a metal one. And she's actually crawled into the stupid thing and is lying down in there. I peer down at her from above.

"I like this one," she says. She looks so pale and frail there, encased in metal, that I actually believe it's possible she could be dead. But the thought is entirely too painful so I push it away, just like the images of Lorelei and Mr. Gomez.

"Metal, Mom, really?"

"This one feels right," Mom says.

JC is looking at Mom, and one of his small baby hands is reaching for her while the other one squeezes the donkey.

"Mom, I don't think you can be in there," I say, my headache pulsing a steady, painful rhythm in my temples.

"This is the one, Julie." The way she says my name makes me cry almost instantly, and my tears drip all over JC, who also starts to cry. So here we are, a couple of sobbing babies standing over Mom in a coffin.

Violet hears us and comes running. She stands beside us looking distressed. "Olive, ma'am, I'm sorry but I'm going to have to insist that you get out." She reaches into an invisible pocket in her purple sweater and produces a tissue like some sort of magician. She hands it to me and I wipe JC's face and blow my nose.

"Thanks," I say.

Neither Violet nor I make a move to help Mom out of the coffin though. She looks strangely at home in there.

"I'm sorry," I say to Violet, or maybe to my mom.

"You know, my mom passed when I was eighteen," Violet says quietly.

I look over at her. Her eyes are cast down to the metal coffin, but she's not really looking at it. Her eyes are unfocused, glazed. "She was such a wonderful woman," Violet says.

There's that word again.

Wonderful.

Maybe it's that everyone draws a blank when they try to sum up a life.

"No, she was more than that," Violet continues.

I nod and crumple the tissue in my hand. I've managed to stop crying, just barely.

"She taught me how to play the piano. She was strict; she made me play my scales every day until I could do it with my eyes closed. But she was so patient with me. I think of her now every time I sit down to play. When I play it's like a prayer." Violet shakes her head and looks at me. I notice that her eyes aren't actually purple; they're light grey.

"I'm sorry," she says.

"No. Don't be. It's nice that you can remember her like that."

Violet helps my mom out of the coffin, smiling sadly. It looks too easy, easier than it should be because my mom weighs almost nothing.

"This is the one," Mom says.

We all linger by the coffin, looking down at it.

"Do you have a partner?" Violet asks Mom.

"My dad," I reply.

"Maybe it would be best if you came back with him. This hardly seems like a decision to made alone." Violet shifts back and forth on her low heels.

"That's a good idea, right, Mom?" I say. JC has stopped crying too. I think he was only crying because I was crying. He's sensitive to other people's feelings, which is sweet, but I hope it doesn't get him beat up when he's older.

"This is the one," Mom says again. Louder this time, more definitive.

"Mom, we have to go home, okay?" I say. "We'll come back with Dad and take a look."

Violet nods solemnly and puts a hand on my shoulder. I smile at her. "Thank you."

"I'm sorry," she says again.

"Me too," I reply.

Then I grab Mom's cold hand and we leave Violet standing alone in the Casket Cathedral.

We drive back through the suburbs and I watch as the sky gets smaller and the streets get more crowded with apartments and houses. As we're approaching our street I turn to my mom.

"Mom, are you sick?" I ask.

She glances over at me briefly and smiles a small smile. More than I've seen from her in days.

"Please, Julie. I'm okay."

Her words feel like a huge relief, but I also know they're a big, fat lie.

"No, you're not. How can you say that?"

"I'm not sick. I'm just . . . tired," she says. "Please."

"You're not sick? Do you promise? Then what's going on? You can tell me. I'm keeping your secret, just like I promised, but I need to know."

"Honestly? I don't know," she whispers. She tightens her grip on the steering wheel. Everything feels heavy—the seatbelt on my chest, the air in the car. JC squeaks his donkey toy, *Hee-haw.*

"I need to know," I whisper back.

"I'm sorry," she says.

"Okay," I say. "Okay."

Then we turn onto our street and there are kids everywhere, walking home from school. It gives me a knot in my stomach and a tingle of panic in my chest. Lorelei is probably on her way home too, and I don't want to have to drive by her, or worse, walk by when we get out of the car.

It's not Lorelei I see when I get home though: it's Henry. He's sitting on our doorstep, fiddling with his backpack. He's wearing these shorts that are a bit too short, and his face is bright with sun. Surprisingly, I'm actually kind of happy to see him. In the midst of all the craziness, he feels like a little island of normal. He smiles when he sees the car pull in and stands up like I've just walked into the room. I get out of the car and grab JC. Mom gets out too and sweeps past Henry without a word or even a glance. He watches her go as if he's thinking of greeting her, but instead he just opens his mouth and nothing comes out.

"Hi," I say. I look around. No Lorelei, thankfully.

"You didn't come back," he says.

"I know, sorry, family emergency."

"Oh. Are you okay?" He shuffles a little bit and squints at me. He's got blue eyes like JC. Like water on a tropical beach.

At this point I'm both tired of holding JC and getting nervous about Lorelei coming by, so I say, "You wanna come in?" Henry nods and shrugs. I guess I should feel weird about having Henry in my house, with my mom acting so strangely, but somehow it feels okay.

After I put JC in his basket in the dining room we head to my room and I shut the door behind us. Henry drops his backpack and starts to walk around touching things like Mom did at the Casket Cathedral.

"Cool room," Henry says.

"I guess," I reply. I kick off my shoes and sit cross-legged on the bed.

"Look, I wanted to say sorry about the party," Henry says as he slides a book off the shelf and flips through it. I recognize this posture and tone. It's his trying-to-be-casual-but-really-super-hyper-aware-of-everything stance.

"What do you mean?" I ask. But I know exactly what he means.

"My hand. Your leg. It was creepy." He puts the book away and continues to circle. His eyes are on everything but me, his shoulders slouching a little more than before.

I laugh. "Yeah, it was."

"I was just happy to be sitting with you, talking to you."

"You didn't seem to care about me before Lorelei shoved me in your face," I say. It comes out angrier than I intended.

"Yeah, well, all that sly crap is sort of an act." He shrugs and looks so defeated I take pity on him and change the subject.

I think about the party, his red-stained lips. "You didn't have any booze."

"I can't stand the stuff."

"Yeah, the beer was nasty. I don't know how Lorelei even drinks it." When I say Lorelei's name again I clam up. Everything goes still and I try hard to push her face out of my mind.

He takes a seat in my desk chair and spins around. For a second he looks like he's having such a good time that I think he's kind of cute. I wonder what it would feel like to have a crush on him. It's hard to imagine loving anyone but Lorelei, but it's not like I'm opposed to having a crush on a guy. Maybe I'm not fully gay after all.

He stops spinning and looks at me, smiling. "So what do you like, stuff-wise?" he asks. It's a completely awkward question given our previous conversation, but it's kind of endearing, so I want to indulge him.

I uncross and re-cross my legs while I try to think. "Um, reading and graphic design, and death," I say. The truth is I threw the death part in to try to be cool, but I don't really like death. Who does?

Henry's face lights up. "My dog died a month ago!" he says. Then he pauses and his face falls.

"That sucks," I say.

"Yeah," he replies.

And in that moment I want nothing more than to tell him everything about my mom. I promised I wouldn't tell Dad, but does that promise extend to friends too? Is Henry even my friend? I shake off the thought. Why would I want to tell Henry anything? What a stupid idea.

Then my cell rings and the noise is so loud it fills the whole room. My ringtone sounds like an old-fashioned phone. We both look over at it at the same time. The knot in my stomach folds itself a little tighter and my tension headache flares up again. I don't even want to think about Lorelei right now.

Brrrrrring. Brrrrrring. Brrrrrring.

"Aren't you going to answer it?" Henry asks.

"No." I know it's Lorelei, and I don't want anything to do with her.

The ringing stops but the sound of it is still in my ears, so I just try to ignore it and focus on Henry.

"So, what kind of stuff do *you* like?" I ask.

He's spinning on the chair again. He stops and looks at me.

"Um, I like soccer and history and . . . you." He grins really wide, and then my cellphone starts going crazy with texts, which totally distracts me from the embarrassment of what he just said. I guess Lorelei got sick of calling.

Henry looks at my phone, then back at me. "It might be important," he says.

"You can check it if you want, but I'm not," I reply. I can't bear the thought of seeing her texts right now.

He shrugs, then actually grabs my phone.

"Hmm . . . ," he says. "You know, you should consider password-protecting your phone. Anyone can just check your messages if they want."

I shrug. Since Lorelei and I normally talk on the phone I don't usually have many messages to protect.

"It's Lorelei," he says. Her name feels like a needle in the heart. As if it could have been anyone else. He squints at the phone and his eyes go wide. "Wow, she's really freaking out. So many exclamation points."

I have the urge to dive under the covers and hide. Instead, I just sit really stiffly, frozen like a corpse, and stare at Henry.

"What should I say to her? What did she do?" he asks.

I don't respond. I have absolutely nothing to say to her right now.

"Okay, I'm trying to get her to calm down." He types for a while and then the phone dings again, about fifty million times. "Wow, I guess that didn't work. Okay, I'm telling her you're busy right now hanging out with me and you'll call her when you can."

I shrug and he glances up at me. He finishes typing something else and the phone dings a couple more times. Then he puts it down gently on the desk and comes to sit beside me. He doesn't try to touch me or anything, thankfully.

"She's still frantic," he says. "She must have done something really bad this time."

It takes a minute for all of my frozen bits to melt, but eventually I say, "What do you mean?"

"Well, when I was dating her she was always doing really shitty stuff like refusing to take my calls or telling people stuff about me behind my back. Once I even heard she made out with some college kid, but she never admitted it."

I want to turn around and say yes a bunch of times

and hug Henry; I want to tell him everything Lorelei has ever done and why it hurts even more because I love her. But instead I just say, "Wow."

"Yeah," he replies.

A few seconds go by and everything is quiet. And I want more than anything to change the subject, so I ask, "Do you believe in heaven?"

"No," he says. "It seems like such a stupid idea— the clouds aren't thick enough to hold people up."

I laugh. "I think it's supposed to be a state of mind."

"I like reincarnation, I think. I'd want to come back as something cool, like a shark or a lion," Henry says.

"I'd want to come back as a baby, like JC," I say, leaning back on my hands so my palms squish into the bed. "He's got it made. He just lies around all day and gets fed and he doesn't have to deal with any stupid drama." I would give anything to trade places with JC right now.

"Yeah, but babies have to grow up," Henry says.

Downstairs I hear the door slam. It's Dad. He's home pretty early today.

"Do you want to stay for dinner?" I ask.

"Really? Are you sure it's okay?" he asks.

"Yeah. You can eat my mom's portion if there's not enough." Because Mom hasn't been eating nearly enough lately. "Do you need to ask your parents or something?"

He shakes his head. "Naw, my dad doesn't really care."

"Cool," I say.

"Cool," he replies.

8.

I was eight when my Grandpa James died. I'd never been to a funeral before, except for Harry the Hamster's. There was this tight pain in my chest for the whole day. Everything in the funeral home was beige and black, and the air smelled like rotten flowers. In the cemetery we watched the coffin go into the ground. I was standing beside my mom and I reached out to hold her hand. I said, "It's all right to cry, Mom." And she did—for hours, for days, for weeks. Grandpa James left a bigger empty space than Harry.

Dinner with Henry is not as awkward as I thought it would be. We order pizza because Mom is too busy staring at her hands to make anything. We're having more and more pizza lately.

We all sit around the table and Henry takes a single slice onto his plate. He eats daintily, taking tiny bites. Not what I expected.

"So, Henry," Dad says, "how's school?"

Dad's trying to act jovial, but he's obviously really tired, because he's kind of hunched in his chair and he's eating really slowly. At least he's making an effort, whereas Mom is just business as usual, quiet and withdrawn, pushing food around her plate and taking only the tiniest of bites. I guess I should be nervous about Henry seeing her that way, but he's not like Lorelei; I don't think he'll get all freaked out. Plus, he's never met Mom before, so he doesn't even know she's not acting normal.

"It's going well. I'm not doing too bad. I'm on the soccer team, which is great," Henry says.

Dad smiles. He's not at his laptop tonight. I guess he'll forego work for guests. "Olive and I used to play soccer together, right, honey?" He looks over at Mom, but she's too busy poking her pizza with a fork. Dad sighs. "Sorry about her, Henry. She's just so tired lately because of the baby. Me too. They've been driving me pretty hard at work."

"That's okay," Henry says. He's eating one slice of pizza for every two I eat. It's kind of embarrassing how polite he is about it.

Mom says nothing. Of course. A piece of her straggly hair has fallen over her face and Dad reaches out to tuck it behind her ear. It's such a tender gesture it makes me feel sick with sadness. It's the first time I've seen him touch her in what—months? It's all I can do not to burst into tears. I wonder if Mr. Gomez tucks Lorelei's hair behind her ear like that? I push my plate away, my appetite gone.

"Done already?" Dad says. "There's so much pizza left."

We've only eaten like half the box, but that's because Mom hasn't even finished one slice. "Mom should have the rest," I say.

Henry pushes his plate away too, his second slice only partially eaten.

I push it back toward him. "You're not done."

"I'm full," he says.

I don't believe him, but I let it slide. I don't want him to feel weird, eating all alone in front of my parents. Henry pushes his chair back from the table and it gives a loud creak. I laugh. "Sorry, the house is old."

"I like it—it's got character," he replies.

"That's what Olive thinks," Dad says, "but I can't stand the noise."

Henry tries to smile at my mom about the thing they have in common, but she's not paying any attention. "Well," he says, "I should probably go. Thanks so much for dinner."

"Sorry we couldn't feed you something more substantial," Dad says.

"No worries," Henry replies.

Then they shake hands in this exaggerated, clapping, manly sort of way, which is pretty funny because Dad is so big and Henry's so small next to him.

"Bye, Mrs. Nolan," Henry says to my mom.

"Olive!" Dad practically yells.

Mom looks up for a second, and I think I see a ghost of a smile on her face, but it may have just been a trick of the light.

I walk Henry out and we sit on my front steps for a bit. It's dark now and there's a cool breeze blowing through the trees. I glance over at Henry. He's just sort of staring out at the street.

"So I guess I was gonna ask you to the dance," he says.

I'm caught off guard, even though I knew this was coming.

"Um . . . well . . . I'm not actually sure I'm going because there's some drama at home and stuff, so . . . " I immediately feel bad for saying that, but all I can think about is Lorelei and me, swaying on the dance floor in each other's arms. Then the image cuts to Lorelei and Mr. Gomez, face to face on his desk, and I'm so grossed out I want to scream, or puke, or both.

"Oh," he says, "yeah, that's cool." He says it really quickly though, like he's trying to cover his embarrassment. His shoulders slump a little and I almost feel bad for him.

"But if I do go, we can go together . . . alone," I offer.

Henry's shoulders square immediately and his gaze finally travels over to me. "Really?"

"Yeah, sure, it would be fun." The last thing I want right now is to go to the dance with Lorelei.

"Cool."

"So anyway, I won't be at school tomorrow," I say, changing the subject before he has time to get too gushy about it.

Henry looks over at me. "Why not?"

Because I can't face Lorelei and Mr. Gomez. I can't imagine what I would say to either of them if they tried to talk to me, tried to convince me that what I saw wasn't real. Because I don't know what's happening with my mom and the whole situation is stressing me out completely. "I don't feel so hot. I'm just tired. I need a sick day or two."

He nods knowingly. "I can grab your homework for you."

"I don't want you to go to any trouble." I don't want to lead him on or anything. I'm not sure I want to go to the dance at all, and now I think he's probably expecting me to.

"Please. I want to, Julie," he says. And there's something in his voice that makes me feel like he would completely understand anything I told him.

I smile. "Okay, sure. Thanks."

. . .

The next morning I tell Dad I feel sick and I don't want to go to school. He seems pretty distracted and agrees to call in sick for me when he gets to work. I sit with him while he wolfs down his breakfast and we don't really talk much because we're both somewhere far away. It's peaceful. The air smells like coffee and Mom is still upstairs in her room, so we have the dining room all to ourselves.

"I like Henry," Dad says eventually.

"Yeah," I reply.

I've never told my dad about my feelings for Lorelei; that's something I've only confessed to Mom.

"Do you think he might be boyfriend material?"

I laugh so hard I snort. Henry being boyfriend material is the last thing on my mind right now. But would it really be that bad? The thought of not being with Lorelei makes my heart hurt too much to even consider it.

"Wow, you're really not into him, huh?" Dad asks.

"I don't think so, Dad," I say.

He holds up his hands. "Okay. Whatever you say."

I roll my eyes at him and stick out my tongue. Then I give a little cough to drive home the fact that I'm not feeling well. But Dad doesn't seem to notice; he's too busy finishing off his breakfast and looking at his phone.

"No rest for the wicked," he murmurs.

Then I leave him to head back up to my room.

• • •

During my "sick" days I mostly just mope around in my room, hiding from my mom and ignoring Lorelei's phone calls until Henry brings my homework. Mr. Gomez writes little "get well soon" notes with smiley faces on my history notes, so I figure he's really trying to butter me up. I hate it and scribble his notes out as soon as I see them. Henry usually hangs out for a bit when he makes the drops. We sit around on my front steps or in the park and talk about nothing in particular: school gossip and movies and soccer and stuff like that. It's kind of nice talking to someone who isn't Lorelei, even though it makes me feel like a traitor to think that. Henry is relaxing; I don't feel like I have to impress him and there's nothing hanging in the air between us. I mean, I know he likes me and everything, but he doesn't make a big deal out of it.

It's Wednesday and I've been "sick" for three days. I'm in my room doing some homework when I hear a voice in my doorway that makes me sick to my stomach.

"Your mom looks really weird," Lorelei says.

I'm frozen in place, horrified that not only is Lorelei here but also that she's seen my mom. I knew she would get freaked if she found out about my mom—that's why I never told her. If I wasn't frozen I would whip my head around and yell at her to get out, but instead I focus on the word *virus* in my text-book. I focus so hard I feel as though I could actually become the word. And I kind of wish I would, right this second.

"I tried knocking, and the front door was unlocked. Your mom was just sitting there, staring at her hands. She didn't even look up. Is she okay?" Lorelei asks.

I try to stay focused on *virus*, just trying not to puke. But then the word starts to look really ridiculous. I want to laugh about it all of a sudden, because who decided it should look that way: with the *v* first and the *s* at the end? I'm not even sure it makes any sense at all.

"Julie?" Lorelei asks.

I don't look up. I hear her flip off her shoes and move over to the bed, the slight creak of her butt pressing into the mattress. Then I hear a sob and that does it. My heart hurts for her, and I can't just ignore her while she cries. I get up and go sit beside her and touch my shoulder to hers.

"I hate that you won't talk to me," she says. She takes her hand and wipes it across her face, under her nose. Then she sniffs—a big, snotty snort. "I was failing history, and Father would kill me if I failed anything, so I asked Mr. Gomez what I could do, and he was just helping me, that's all." She looks at the floor as she explains, and I'm not sure what to say. I don't know if it's true or not, but I really want it to be true. What did I see, really? I try to think back to that moment. Mr. Gomez looking down at Lorelei with what—pity? I thought it was lust, love even. But now I'm not so sure.

"Why didn't you tell me?" I ask. She'd mentioned struggling in math a bit, but she never made it seem serious. I certainly didn't know she was flunking history. What else hasn't she told me?

"Because I was embarrassed. Father said he might send me away for school, so I was freaking out." Her eyes are rimmed with red and she's still staring at the floor.

"What do you mean, send you away for school?"

"Boarding school—Father wants to send me because he says I lack focus. Math, history, science—all of them are going down the drain." She's stopped crying completely now but her words are coming out in meek little squeaks.

"He can't send you away! It's not fair," I say.

She finally looks at me. "He can do whatever he wants. He's in charge."

"What about your mom?" I almost reach out and grab her hand, but then I stop myself. I don't know if I believe her yet.

"Mother will do whatever Father wants. She's a pushover," Lorelei says. "But I just have to get through high school and then . . . "

"And then what?" I say. "What about university?"

She shrugs. "Maybe I won't even go. I'm not like you, Julie. I'm stupid."

The word hits me hard: *stupid*.

"How can you say that?" I ask.

I can't believe that Lorelei is anything less than confident in everything she does.

She looks at me and I see it in her eyes—she believes it. She thinks she's stupid.

"Because it's true. But it's okay. I have other things going for me, right?" She wiggles her boobs a bit and laughs, even though we both know it's not funny.

"You're not stupid."

"Julie, I'm almost failing most of my classes. I'm not kidding that I'm going to get sent away."

"I wish you had told me. I could have helped you. I could still help you."

She shrugs. "I didn't want to worry you, dahling."

Her *dahling* falls flat.

"Look, you won't tell, will you? About me needing extra help?" Lorelei asks. She reaches out and grabs my hand. Our clasped hands rest on my leg.

Who would I tell? Plus, I'm already keeping my mom's secret, so why not Lorelei's too?

"No, I won't tell," I say.

I stare at our hands and think about how nice they look together. How much I love holding hands with her. How much I lov*ed* holding hands with her? Nothing feels right anymore, but I want it to get back to where it was. I'm already losing enough in my life. I can't lose her too.

"I miss you, Julie. Let's just forget about all of this and be us again."

I nod, but I don't know what to say.

"Let's go to the dance together, please?" she says. "Let's just be normal."

That's what I wanted, right? All I ever wanted? I can't tell if she's trying to manipulate me. I can't tell if I'm trying to manipulate myself. But I nod again and she leans in to hug me. Her breath is hot in my ear. I used to live for that feeling, but in this moment it just makes me sad.

"Okay," I reply.

"I should go," she says softly.

"I can help you," I say again. I force a smile and she smiles back.

"Don't forget the funeral Friday," she says. I wince. I had forgotten. I can't imagine going to some random person's funeral right now and listening to the eulogy. But I don't want to let Lorelei down. I said I would go. I nod and she slips off the bed and disappears out into the creaky hall.

. . .

When I go down for dinner, Dad isn't home and Mom's just heated up gross leftover pizza in the microwave. We sit together in the silent dining room and I eat too fast because I can't stand just sitting in the quiet. What did we used to talk about before Mom changed? I try to think of all the conversations we used to have about work, about school, but nothing in particular comes to mind.

"Lorelei and I made up," I say.

There's this long pause as Mom slowly peels a piece of pepperoni off her pizza. The cheese is like a greasy bit of glue that holds on tight to the meat.

"You were fighting?"

"We kissed," I say. Because I'm feeling like I have to fill the grey air with something and it might as well be words.

"That's nice," Mom says.

I want to shake her. This is not my mom. My mom would be excited for me, thrilled. She would ask me a million embarrassing questions and I would pretend to be reluctant but I would give her a million embarrassing answers, because we used to be best friends.

"I just want you to be normal, Mom," I whisper.

She looks up at me, and for a fraction of a second her back straightens and her eyes lose some of their terrible hollowness and she says, "I know." Then she hunches back over her plate and stops doing anything, even poking her pizza, and I know I've lost her again. I suddenly feel too sick and sad to eat anymore, so I just push my plate to the side and run away upstairs to my room to hide.

Later, I text Henry and ask him to meet me. I feel like a walk so we arrange to meet at school.

The air is heavy with almost-rain and the streets are empty because it's still dinnertime and everyone in the neighbourhood is in their houses eating. I can see them through some of the windows on the street: three, four, five to a table, all steaming food and smiles and conversations about their days.

Henry is waiting on the front steps of the school. I stand on the sidewalk and watch him for a second. He's staring up at the sky and he looks so lost in thought I almost hate to interrupt. He likes soccer and history and apparently stargazing too—even though there aren't even that many stars in the city and the sky is partially filled with clouds. Maybe that's all we are: a collection of the things we like and the things we're good at. Maybe that's how we'll all be remembered.

I step forward and walk up the path to the front steps. Henry looks over at me, startled. Then he shouts "Hi!" even though there are only two people here.

"Hi!" I shout too, so he doesn't have to feel awkward and alone in his shouting.

"I brought your homework." He's talking at a more normal volume now as he nods to a plastic bag full of papers leaning against the wall beside him.

"Thanks."

I sit down on the stairs next to him and there is a bit of a pause in the conversation.

Then he says, "So school was crazy today. Sheila beat up this new kid Wesley in the soccer field and got three weeks' detention. But Wesley's dad is a lawyer so everyone's saying they might press charges." Sheila is the school bully. She's tough and angry and just about everyone avoids her—if they can.

"Yeah, well, it would be about time someone got back at her," I say.

Luckily, I've managed to avoid Sheila's wrath so far. She's pretty much the only girl in the school, the only person, for that matter, who does anything physical to anybody else—the rest of the girls just destroy each other with gossip, and most of the guys are pretty tame.

"Yeah, I mean, she did have something coming for all the crap she's pulled," Henry says, looking back up at the sky. It seems like he just can't help himself. I have to admit I think it's kind of cute, all this stargazing.

I watch him for a bit, out of the corner of my eye, then I say, "So, um, anyway, I can't go to the dance with you." It's kind of out of the blue, but I have to say it at some point. Dad says you should tell the truth in the same way you'd rip off a Band-Aid—all at once so it's easy and quick.

There's a long silence from Henry's direction.

"Oh," he says after a while.

"It's just that I promised Lorelei I would go with her because she doesn't have a date, and we decided it a while ago but kind of got into a fight, as you know. But we've made up now, so yeah."

"Okay," he says.

"We can have a dance though—like, a slow one," I say.

"Sure," he replies. "Well, anyway, I brought your homework," he says again, nodding for a second time at the plastic bag full of papers.

"Yeah, you said."

"So I'll see you at school?" he asks.

I guess I have no reason to stay home from school anymore now that everything is okay with Lorelei.

"Yeah. Thanks again for picking this stuff up for me," I say.

"Yeah." He gets up and leaves. He doesn't even look back, and for a second I wish he would because I want to know what colour his eyes are in the streetlight—which is kind of weird, I guess, given that I don't even like him that much. Instead, I just watch him walk away. Then I sit for another minute or two before I grab my stuff and head home.

When I get back to the house Dad still isn't home from work. JC is upstairs with Mom and I'm happy I don't have to deal with either of them. I plan to actually get up for school tomorrow, so I go up to bed and fall asleep almost instantly. I dream of Violet giving a mass at the Casket Cathedral and Lorelei floating out amongst the stars.

The clock says 3:00 a.m. when I hear the banging. I jump out of bed and race out of my room. As soon as I reach the bottom step I'm hit with JC's freshly woken wail coming from the dining room. I run in and flip on the light. Mom's at the table and JC's in his basket. Mom's eyes are wide open and she's staring at nothing. She doesn't even look over at me. I wonder if she sits here every night—or maybe it's only the nights she's not under the bedsheet. I run over to JC and try to coochy-coo him into silence, but it doesn't really work. He just pauses a moment in his wailing to look at me, then starts up again a second later.

Then there's another bang, bang, bang on the door and JC lets out a fresh screech. I jump. For a second I'd forgotten why I came downstairs in the first place.

I go to the door.

It's Mrs. Wellington, who lives two doors down. She's about eighty years old and she's wearing a lacy white nightgown. Her old face is crinkled like a piece of light brown fabric in need of ironing.

"The Lees are on vacation, please help," she says. The Lees are our next-door neighbours, and they're always on vacation.

"What's wrong?" I ask. I open the door wider to let her in and she stumbles a bit. That's when I notice her colour is off: black smudges line her face, her bare arms and legs, even the seams of her nightgown.

"Fire . . . Jerry's in bed, but I couldn't lift him. He told me to get help." Jerry's her husband and he just had hip surgery. I know this because Mom made them a pie before she turned into a zombie, and had me take it to him. Jerry was so happy about it that he made me come into his bedroom and accept a kiss on the cheek from his leathery lips. It freaked me out a little—I guess I didn't want to think that someday I would be that old and helpless.

"Mom?" I say. Mrs. Wellington is clutching my arm and hobbling alongside me as I guide her into the dining room.

"Mom, there's a fire and Jerry's in bed. We have to

call 911!" I say. At the word *fire* she snaps to attention. She suddenly looks like the Mom I know. Alert and vibrant. Was it that particular word? Does she remember who she used to be? A firefighter. A hero.

"Mom, 911, okay? I'm going to wake Dad up," I say. JC is still screaming, but of course everyone's ignoring him. There's a momentary pause where everything seems to go still, and then in one quick, amazing motion Mom is on her feet, streaking past me and running out the open front door. My heart seizes with panic. Where the hell is she going? I can't deal with this right now.

I run to the phone and grab it, then hand it off to Mrs. Wellington.

"Where are you going?" she says, staring at the phone as though she's never seen one before in her life. JC sounds like a siren and the noise is clawing at my stomach, twisting it practically inside out. This can't be happening; I have to go find Mom.

"Just call 911," I say. Then I run out the door, following my mom into the dark, empty street.

So here I am, bare feet on cold grass, watching Mom as she leaps across the Lees' lawn. Despite her lack of eating or sleeping or thinking, she is perfect in her motion: every step like the flap of a wing as she attempts to take flight.

And here is the Wellingtons' house, smouldering

like an early-morning campfire, flames licking at the windows, its edges bowed and bent.

My heart is beating hard against my rib cage as I give chase, and I wonder what I'll do if I catch her. Will I pull her back, my hands on her thin, fragile bones? Will I drag her to the damp ground so we can watch together as Mr. Wellington burns in his bed in the deep recesses of his house?

But I don't get the chance to answer my own questions because here is Mom, fully alive with breath and energy. She pushes open the front door and vanishes into the black and red and orange of the house as tendrils of smoke curl out at first, then pour out faster and faster, like they are billowing out of a dragon's nostril: grey and black and toxic.

Now I'm at the front door, breathless and terrified, peering into the darkness and the light and screaming at the top of my lungs. I shout for my past-tense Mom, whose body is probably being incinerated in this bright, flaming house. Why would she run in there without her equipment? She knows how dangerous it is. Is she operating purely on muscle memory—all the burning houses she's run toward in the past—or is something more sinister going on? Is my mom trying to kill herself? Trying to make it so we all have to speak about her in the past tense?

Mom was *a heroic firefighter.*

I'm standing in the doorway, eyes closed, counting the steps to Mr. Wellington's room.

Counting the obstacles and the inches of muscle on my mom's arms.

Muscle that will have to be enough to pick up the small, broken man and carry him back through the maze of fire and smoke and out into the open air. I'm counting now, the numbers rising into tens and twenties as the wail of sirens joins in and I feel the panicked warmth of my dad behind me.

"She went in!" I shout to him, over the sirens and the roar of the flames. I watch as his face falls and I count: fifty, sixty, too many seconds. The lights are flashing and Dad strains toward the fiery door, but he doesn't follow her in.

It's okay though.

Because here she comes now. Out from the smoke and the flame, clothes singed the colour of ash, hair like wild embers reaching toward the cloudy sky, Mr. Wellington draped over her shoulder like a pale shawl.

Now here I am on the grass with Dad, kneeling beside Mom and Mr. Wellington. Their eyes are closed as if they're dreaming, their chests heaving as though there isn't enough air in the world.

The paramedics and firefighters are swarming like flies, but I'm leaning closer and closer to my mom. And here are Mom's eyes, open now, looking directly at me—not through me but burrowing straight into my soul. And everything in me is wide open as I lean down close and ask, "Mom, are you okay?"

And she replies, "I want the metal one, Julie, promise me."

9.

Lorelei and I met when I was nine years old. It was the first time I'd ever had a best friend that wasn't my mom. It's not like I stopped caring about my mom or anything, it's just that I had new priorities. I started going to sleepovers at Lorelei's house and telling my secrets to someone new. I remember coming home from school one day and my mom asked me how my day was. I could have told her everything, like I always used to, but instead I just said, "Fine." My mom smiled, but it wasn't her usual bright, all-teeth smile. There was a new space between us, in a shape I couldn't recognize.

These bright lights are the hospital. This burn in my throat is some sort of generic-brand soda. I'm on a comfy grey chair and Mom is on a hospital bed beside me, hooked up to an IV and tucked safely away under a baby-blue blanket. With her eyes are closed, Mom looks more like a skeleton than ever. The lines of her bones are sharp and clear and it makes me want to touch them just to feel her skull. It's strange to think that all we are beneath our skin is a bunch of white bones.

Dad is a big bundle of emotions: tired, scared, mad, sad, loving. He hovers around Mom's bedside, periodically touching her face, her arms, her hands. Then he comes over to me and hugs me and strokes my hair, my forehead, my cheeks. JC isn't here. Babies don't belong in hospitals except right when they're born because they're more susceptible to superbugs and other bacterial infections, so we asked our neighbour Mrs. Carmichael to watch him.

The doctors say Mom is fine. It's practically a miracle, seeing as she was in the Wellingtons' house for almost three minutes and you would think she'd be suffering from smoke inhalation or something. But no, nothing except that her hair is a little singed and she has the general smell of bonfire lingering on her skin because she hasn't had the chance to shower yet. It's terrible to see my mom in a hospital bed, but the truth is I'm also a little in awe of her. She was a hero before, but now I'm pretty sure she's a superhero. It might have been reckless to go running into that house without her gear, but it was completely heroic. That's the Mom I know and love.

It's mid-afternoon when Dad goes out for some coffee. A couple of minutes after he leaves, Mom opens her eyes. I'm not sure if she's just waking up or if she only had her eyes closed because Dad was here. I lean over until I'm right in her face. Her breathing is so slight I can't even feel it. Her breath smells like nothing.

"Are you okay?" I ask.

Her eyes look brighter than usual. I even think I see a little of my old mom in there as she almost, almost smiles, but then just nods slightly instead.

"No, I'm dead," she says flatly. Simply.

My entire body grows cold. This is new. This is bad.

"No, you're not. You totally saved Mr. Wellington. Mrs. Wellington was crying and thanking God, then you, and then God again, and the paramedics said you were fine fire-wise but that you were a little dehydrated, which makes sense given the fact that you haven't been eating a lot . . . " Her brown eyes are watching me full on for the first time in a long time. It feels nice to really have her attention, so I keep going. "But anyway, you're going to be fine. You're a hero, Mom. A superhero."

"The dead get buried," she says quietly, as if it's the most reasonable thing in the world.

"No, Mom. You're not dead. Dead people don't talk, and you're talking to me." I pause. There's a pressure building in my chest, a dreadful question bubbling up inside of me. "Is that why you ran into the house?

Do you *want* to be dead?" My fingers are numb with panic. Maybe she wasn't being heroic at all. Maybe she was trying to kill herself.

"No. I was already dead. I'm dead and the dead get buried. Can't you see? My heart is gone." She lifts up her hands to show me her arms, and the spider silk of her IV gleams in the afternoon sunlight.

"You look fine," I say.

"My skin is falling off," she replies. She says it so simply, like there's no arguing the fact.

I look hard, but her skin is still there, fully intact. Although I guess a little blue. My mind is racing as I try to sort all of this out. She thinks she's dead. Wants to be buried. And I have no idea what to do, short of telling Dad, which she told me she doesn't want me to do. I look around the room. I'm in the hospital and my mom is dead. I should tell somebody, somebody who is not Dad.

"Maybe we should tell the nurse?" I ask.

"Nurse?" Mom narrows her eyes and looks like she's trying hard to understand exactly what that word means.

"Yes!" I'm getting excited now. "This is perfect! You don't want to tell Dad, but we could tell someone else. How about the nurse? She's so nice." I give my mom my most pleading expression, although I'm pretty sure it won't have its desired effect.

"The nurse," Mom whispers, staring off into the space above my head. "The nurse will tell your dad."

She very well might. Is she bound by some sort of law to do that? I sigh and throw my head back in frustration. I want to yell at the ceiling, but instead I press my lips together and look back at Mom. Why won't she just let me tell Dad? Are they in some sort of fight, or is she really just worried for him because he's been working so hard?

"Okay, well, I need you to snap out of it then. I need you to be my mom again. Let's just drop this whole dead thing, please? If you won't let me tell anyone, you at least have to try to work with me here." Mom trusted me with her secret and I'm not going to let her down. But I need her to at least try to get better. I need her to try to be my mom again. I'm shaking a bit as I reach out and grab her hands.

"Okay?" I ask.

"Okay," she whispers. But I'm not even sure she knows what she's agreeing to.

At this point Dad comes back, his hands full of paper cups and bags of doughnuts. When he sees Mom's eyes open he rushes over and shoves all the food into my hands. Then he grabs Mom's arm and starts crying. He gushes with these big, loud, horrible sobs that are actually worse than Mom's quiet nothingness. I back out of the room and go sit in the hallway.

I eat a maple cream doughnut and try to listen to anything else but the sound of my dad crying.

When we finally leave the hospital that night there are a handful of reporters in the main lobby. They're snapping pictures. They ask questions at exactly the same time so all the words jumble together and sound like a buzz. Mom stays completely quiet and Dad says, "No comment."

On the way home we're all quiet. I want to say something to break the silence, but I can't think of anything.

After a while Dad looks at me in the rear-view mirror. "Are you okay, Julie?"

"Um, yeah, why?"

"It's just that I'm sorry I didn't wake up sooner." His voice wavers and he pauses. I look at him in the mirror. His eyes are all red and bloodshot. He's so tired, so overworked, overstressed. I feel so bad for him. Maybe this is exactly how Mom feels too. This is the reason she won't tell him her secret.

"I'm throwing out those damn earplugs . . . but I'm sure it must have been traumatic for you. I'm so sorry. It's been so stressful." Dad's rambling, and I really want to say something to make him feel better.

"I'm okay, Dad, really."

"Are you sure?"

"Yeah, I mean, I guess it's a little weird to have a superhero mom, but it's cool too, you know?"

Dad sighs. He watches the road for a bit, then glances back at me in the mirror. "Julie, your mom is not a superhero. She shouldn't have gone into that house."

"But if she didn't Mr. Wellington would be dead," I say.

"Yes, but your mom has a responsibility to you and JC." He sighs heavily and his shoulders droop a bit. "It was irresponsible of her to put her life at risk like that. At work she has proper equipment and backup to mitigate risk. But she didn't have any of that at the Wellingtons'."

It's strange to talk about Mom like she's not here.

"You always tell me to do the right thing," I say.

Dad sighs again, and he's starting to sound pretty dramatic. "Sometimes the right thing is debatable. Leaving you and JC isn't the right thing."

"And you, she would be leaving you too," I say.

"And me." Dad's voice drops to a tired whisper.

"So she should have let Mr. Wellington die?" I ask.

He doesn't look at me in the mirror this time; he just keeps his eyes on the road. "I don't know, Julie."

"Would you have left him in there to die?" I ask.

This time Dad does look at me in the mirror again, long and hard. "I don't know," he repeats.

"Well, me neither," I say, "but doesn't that just make Mom even more of a superhero, because when she was faced with that question she chose no?"

Dad laughs, but it's not his usual merry laugh. It's kind of nervous and shaky. "Maybe, honey. I don't know."

When we get home Mrs. Carmichael opens the door to greet us like she actually lives in our house and is expecting us for dinner. Dad thanks her while I help Mom upstairs to her room. Mom is no longer moving like she did on the lawn: no more leaping, just small, tentative steps like she turned ninety-nine years old overnight. Her arm feels like bone as I help her lie down in bed. She looks at me for a minute, then turns her attention to the ceiling fan.

"You're a superhero, Mom," I say. I kiss her on the forehead, then head down to grab JC and put him to bed. When I'm done, Dad and I sit at the dining-room table for a bit. We open a bag of chips and eat straight out of the bag.

"Your mom's agreed to go to therapy. I know she's not been herself lately. I think she just needs a little help," Dad says. He looks tired as he digs around in the bag. The crinkling of plastic fills in all the silences.

I feel a tingle of relief flitter through me. It's hard being the only one keeping Mom's secret. Now maybe she can share it with someone else. Hopefully she'll tell the therapist everything and it will all be out in the open and I won't have to hold on to everything by myself anymore. "Good," I say.

"I really want to be here for her, and you and JC, right now. I'm sorry I've been so lost in work. It's been causing some tension between me and Olive too . . . I'm sorry."

He never calls her Olive. It's strange how both of my parents are treating me like an adult right now. They never used to share secrets or talk about their relationship. The chips are salt and vinegar and the acidic taste fills my whole head. "It's okay, Dad. I mean, are you and Mom . . . okay?"

"I don't know, it's just . . . " He shakes his head. "You shouldn't have to worry about all this stuff. You should be going on dates and taking tests and rebelling, you know, being a teenager."

I sigh. "Being a teenager is overrated."

"Is everything okay? At school?"

There are crumbs everywhere. I sweep some off the table and onto the floor. I have a small cut on my finger and the vinegar bites it. In all the chaos I've barely had time to think about anything else. Lorelei and Mr. Gomez—what I did or didn't see. Henry and the Spring Fling. But it all seems so small right now.

"It's fine, Dad. Seriously, don't worry about me."

He rubs his hands through his hair. There's a spray of grey in there that I never noticed before.

"Look, there's something else too." He sounds stressed and I hold my breath, preparing myself for who-knows-what bad news. "They want me to go down to L.A. for a bit. I'm leaving tomorrow."

I exhale. Okay, I can handle this. I've just got to take care of Mom like I've been doing. Make sure she doesn't run into any more burning buildings. "They didn't say how long?"

"Maybe a week. Maybe less. I'm sorry about this, honey. I want to be here, but I have to keep working. I just have to."

"I know," I say. "It's fine. We'll be fine." I feel like I'm trying to convince myself too. "You should get some sleep." I fold the chip bag and stand up. My chair creaks.

Dad grins. "Did you fart?"

I laugh and kiss him on the forehead.

Back in my bedroom I call Lorelei. I don't even really want to talk to her right now, but I want something to distract me from all the thoughts swirling through my brain. When she picks up she's laughing.

"What's funny?" I ask.

"Nothing, just some cat pictures online," she replies.

I hear some typing in the background on her end and something dings softly. Is she chatting with someone right now? I try to remember if she's even into cat pictures.

"Cool." I lean back on my bed and turn my attention toward her, trying to ignore the dings.

"What's up? You missed school again today," Lorelei says. She sounds distracted. Sometimes she gets like this and it drives me crazy. Maybe I'm too needy though. I guess I shouldn't expect to always have her all to myself.

I should tell her about Mom.

"Nothing much," I reply instead. I'd like to say that I'm not telling her because I don't want to talk about it anymore. But the truth is I just don't want to talk to *her* about it. It's a strange feeling because I used to want to talk to her all the time, but everything just feels different now.

"Well, you missed a dance committee meeting. But don't worry, I can get you all caught up tomorrow," Lorelei says.

"Do you think there are different kinds of love?" I ask, "Or, like, just one kind?" I know it's a stupid question, but I need to know whether you can love someone without telling them your secrets. Like Mom with Dad, or me with Lorelei.

"Wow . . . um . . . I don't know," Lorelei says.

"Sorry, I was just wondering."

"Well, there's family love and then lover love and stuff, so yeah, for sure there are." I picture her sitting cross-legged at her desk, surrounded by her yellow walls.

"Yeah, I guess. Do you think you would save someone from a burning building if you knew they were probably going to die if you didn't?" I ask.

She doesn't answer for a long moment. Then she says, "Are you okay, Julie?" I hear the soft ding of a text again in the background.

"Are you talking to someone else right now?"

She laughs. "What is this, twenty questions?"

"Sorry."

We both go quiet for a second, and the clicking and dinging continues on her end. I wonder again what she's doing, but I don't want to be all prying and needy.

"We can just talk tomorrow if you want," I say.

"Okay, get some sleep. You sound tired."

"Yeah, I guess I am."

There's a long pause while I continue to listen to the clicks of her keyboard.

"You still there?" she asks after a bit.

"Yeah."

"Okay, I'll see you tomorrow. Sorry, I'm a bit distracted right now," she adds as an afterthought.

"Yeah, okay . . . bye, Lorelei."

"Bye." She hangs up then and everything is silent on the other end of the line. For a minute I consider calling her back and telling her everything. Instead, I text Henry.

> Julie: You up?
> Henry: Yeah, what's up?

I pause for a second and stare at the screen. I just realized this is the first time we've talked since we were at the school together and I told him I couldn't go to the dance with him. Now I'm feeling pretty awkward about texting him at all.

> Julie: Sorry.
> Henry: What for?
> Julie: Texting I guess?
> Henry: Why?

I sit straight up now, legs crossed, because I'm feeling nervous. I stick my feet underneath my legs so far that they start to tingle.

> Julie: Because of the dance thing. I kind of forgot.

I picture him in his room, looking at his phone, even though I've never actually seen his room.

Henry: Whatever. We're still friends right?

I breathe deeply and shake a bit on the inhale because I'm super relieved he's being so cool.

Julie: Yes. :)
Henry: Do you want to meet up or something?
         Like in the park?
Julie: Now?

I look around as though something in my room might object to me going to park.

Henry: Yeah, I just want to get out for a bit.
Julie: Okay.

So in about fifteen minutes we're together, in the park, on the swings. It's a clear night and all these stars are poking holes in the sky, way more than usual. We sit for a while in silence and stare up at them. Henry seems enthralled, but I can't stop thinking about the dark doorway of the Wellingtons' house, about my mom bounding across the neighbours' lawn.

Then all of a sudden Henry says, "Isn't it wild that we're sitting on the surface of this planet and there's, like, a trillion other planets out there that might have kids like us on their surfaces?"

And in that moment, I realize that I don't want to tell my secrets to Lorelei but I do want to tell them to Henry, so I say, "My mom is a superhero and I think I'm gay, or at least half gay."

Then he turns his face to the sky and whispers so quietly I can barely hear, "My dad hasn't really talked to me since my mom died."

His words hit me hard and I don't know what to say.

So we just swing. We swing higher and higher in perfect pendulum arches like a couple of old grandfather clocks. We swoosh and swing and open our mouths to the spring air and our eyes are filled with stars and hazy park light. When I look over at Henry he's smiling at the sky. After a long time we slow down and stop in tandem.

"So what do you mean your mom is a superhero?" Henry asks.

It's weird to hear his voice after so much silence.

"She saved this guy last night, our neighbour, in a fire. She just went into the burning house and pulled him out," I say. "I mean, she was always a hero because she's a firefighter, but this was some new level of awesome." I try to reconcile the image of her bounding across the lawn with the person who thinks she's dead. It was like I got her back for a second, and then she vanished again.

"Wow. I didn't know she was a firefighter. That's cool."

"Yeah. And the freaky thing is that I saw her do it. I mean, I wasn't in the house or anything—do you think you'd go into a burning house to save someone?"

"I want to say yes, but I'd probably be too scared," Henry says. He kicks the dirt a little, revealing deeper and darker parts underneath.

"Yeah, me too. I mean, I *was* too scared and I didn't go in. I was right there at the door and I didn't do anything. I think I'm a coward."

He shrugs. "I think you're just a normal person. Most people wouldn't go. It's so dangerous. I mean, she could have died."

"Yeah, I know. She usually has gear, and backup . . . but I guess my mom has extenuating circumstances," I say.

I both want him to ask and don't want him to ask about my mom's extenuating circumstances. I mean, I wouldn't actually tell him about the dead thing. At the same time, I would want the option of telling him if he asked me directly.

He doesn't ask though, which I kind of think is nice because it means he doesn't want to pry, and it makes me feel super fond of him right in that moment.

So I say, "Do you want to hold hands?"

He reaches out his hand and I grasp it.

We are connected: two separate swings, two different lives, one line of hand and arm reaching across the sand.

"It's not sexual though, okay?" I say. "Because I'm kind of really in love with Lorelei, actually . . . I think." It's the first time I've ever told that to anyone besides my mom. But it just felt right.

He sighs. "I know how that is. But she's a bit flighty, so be careful."

His hand feels sturdy.

"Why doesn't your dad talk to you?" I ask.

His grip loosens for a second. Then it tightens again and he keeps looking forward toward the street.

"I don't know. I've asked him, but he never really responds other than shrugging or grunting or something. Maybe I remind him too much of my mom. Or maybe he just has nothing to say."

He's talking quietly, like the words are hard to speak, and I nod like I know what he's talking about, but I don't at all. I don't know what to say, but I feel like I have to say something. "I'm sorry."

I guess it should feel weird talking to Henry about all of this stuff, but it doesn't. We have told each other more tonight than I've ever told Lorelei, but somehow it all feels natural, normal, right.

"The worst part is that he doesn't do anything around the house. He manages to go to work, but that's about it. When he gets home he just watches TV then goes to bed. I feed myself, do all the cleaning. I'm sure you've noticed my dirty shirts," he says, clutching at the corner of his shirt. "I haven't done laundry for a bit. Maybe your superhero mom can come and save me," Henry says, laughing. "From the silent treatment."

"Maybe," I reply. I'm trying to picture her breaking down Henry's door and whipping his dad into shape, but it's not really working for me. "So far she's been more of an emergency-rescue kind of hero though. I'm not sure she's into psychological interventions."

"I was just joking," Henry says, giving my hand a quick squeeze.

"Oh yeah. Right. But either way, you should do something. Can't you report him to children's services for neglect or something?"

He looks over at me and tightens his grip on my hand, not in a threatening way, but in a scared way— it's all hot and getting sticky. "You can't tell anyone, okay?" he says. "He just needs time. That's all."

More secrets, but I'm good at keeping them, I think. I'm actually kind of proud. I'm a vault: dead mom, Lorelei's crappy grades, neglected Henry Carter.

I nod. "Okay."

"Do you wanna try swinging together?" he asks.

"Okay," I say again.

And so we do, holding hands across the space between us. Lips curled into smiles the shape of crescent moons. Feeling both adult and childlike in the fresh spring night air. We climb higher and higher, and when we get to the top Henry opens his mouth really wide and whoops into the sky. The next time around I do it too, and we stay there for who knows how long, swinging and whooping like idiots, still holding hands against the backdrop of the stars.

10.

When I was ten I insisted Mom take me to the hairdresser because I wanted to cut all my hair off. I had been growing it since I was eight. When we got there the stylist sighed as she ran her fingers through my hair. "But it's so beautiful and long! Girls shouldn't have short hair—are you sure you want to cut it all?" she said. Before I knew what was happening my mom was dragging me out of the salon and back home, where she plopped me down and cut my hair herself. She said, "Don't ever let anyone tell you how a girl should be."

So the next day Dad's gone to La La Land. That's what he calls L.A. when he's feeling playful. Meanwhile, Mom has been sitting at the dining-room table like she's waiting for someone to serve her dinner. She hasn't been to the shrink yet because her appointment is on Saturday, but I wonder what she'll act like in her sessions. If I were the shrink and Mom came in to see me I'd immediately know something was wrong and give her medication or something, probably Zoloft. That's what Paul Xi had to take when he had a breakdown at the beginning of the school year and tried to cut his wrists in the washroom. They took him away for three weeks. When he came back he was pretty chill and he said his parents gave him Zoloft. Sheila threatened to beat him up if he didn't share, but he said his parents kept the pills in a locked box on the top shelf in the kitchen so there was no sharing to be had. It's a shame though, because I think Sheila might need some Zoloft herself.

While I'm eating breakfast the phone rings and breaks the silence. I look over at Mom but she doesn't look up, so I wait for a few more rings then get up to answer it.

"Hello?"

"I'm looking for Olive Nolan?"

I hear the sound of chaos in the background. "Can I ask who's calling?"

"This is Myra Wilson from the *Toronto Sun*. Are you Julie?"

"Um, yeah?"

"Great! So is your mom home, hon?"

Myra doesn't sound that much older than me, but somehow her calling me hon makes me feel comfortable. I look over at my mom, but she doesn't look at me; she's blankly staring off into the hall. "Sorry, she can't come to the phone right now."

"Well, I was just looking to talk to her about the other night, the fire—were you there?"

I don't know how to answer that. Of course I was. I close my eyes and see that dark doorway my mom vanished into, remember the tightness in my chest as I counted the seconds, minutes she was in there.

"I don't have any comment," I say instead.

Myra laughs. "Wow, you were prepped for this, huh?"

I smile apologetically into the phone. "Sorry."

"It's okay. I'll try to get a hold of her some other time. She's a real hero, Julie. You should be proud."

"I am," I reply.

"Can I quote you on that?" she asks. Then she laughs again before she says goodbye.

The phone rings a couple more times before I leave for school. More newspapers. I say "no comment" to all of them.

Before I leave I make Mom promise to take JC to the park. I hate leaving her alone, but I do have to go back to school at some point.

"Babies are like plants—they need sunshine to grow," I say. She doesn't really respond, but she does look at me, so that's something, I guess. She's been even quieter than usual since the fire, so I'm just as excited as Dad is for her to go to the shrink. "Don't talk to anyone when you go though," I warn her. I don't want her being grilled by nosy reporters when I'm not there to say "no comment" for her.

When I arrive at school Henry's hanging out on the front steps, and it looks like he's waiting for something. He smiles when he sees me and stands up, so I guess it's me he's waiting for.

"Hey," he says, then he hands me a newspaper.

"Hey," I say back. I look at said newspaper and am surprised to see me and Mom and Dad on the front page under the big bold title "FIREFIGHTING HERO." The article is all about Mom. I don't have time to read it though, because the bell rings for class and I have to go in.

"Just a heads-up," Henry says.

"Thanks," I reply.

We walk together until the hall splits off and he goes one way and I go another. I'm almost sad to see him go. At the beginning of the year I was super happy that I didn't have any classes with him, but now I wish I had at least one.

Once I'm alone I start to clue in that people are looking at me funny: with a reverence that is mostly reserved for famous people. I check out the picture on the front of the paper again: it's us leaving the hospital last night. I'm partially obscured by Dad's arm, and the part of me you can see looks frazzled. Not the most flattering media debut.

On my way to class, Nima Dorje and Gwen Cooper corner me. I share a couple of classes with them, but they've never seemed interested in me before. Now they're acting like we're best friends. I think Lorelei might be friends with them, but that's not saying much, because she's friends with everyone.

"Hey, Julie, how's it going?" Nima says. She's acting casual, leaning against the lockers in the same way I lean against the bathroom wall when I'm trying to be casual with Lorelei.

"Hi." I'm still holding onto the newspaper and I try to tuck it behind my back because I don't want to seem like an egomaniac.

"So you were there that night, right?" Gwen asks. At least she gets right to the point. I want to say "no comment" to them too, but I feel like that might not go over so well. It's weird that the only reason these girls are talking to me is because of my mom. It feels so painfully disingenuous.

I give them a big, fake smile and nod enthusiastically. "Yeah, it was pretty crazy."

"You've *got* to tell us about it—maybe at lunch?" Nima asks.

"Maybe," I say. I'm trying to be diplomatic as I inch toward the door to my classroom.

"It's a date, then," Nima says, grinning.

"Actually, I promised Lorelei I'd eat with her today, so maybe another time?"

Nima and Gwen look disappointed, and I feel bad for a minute before I remember they don't really care about *me*. I give them a quick wave and a smile before I run off.

I get to class a few minutes late. Mr. Gomez smiles at me really wide, like he's trying to show off a new bleach job on his teeth or something. It's my first day back since I ran away from him and Lorelei, so I kind of feel awkward about seeing him. I mean, I believe Lorelei and everything, but I still wonder about the way Mr. Gomez was looking at her that day. He looked so lusty and predatory. An eagle diving for a mouse on the ground. If he's actually into her then it's pretty gross.

Everyone else grins at me too. Everyone except Lorelei. She doesn't even look in my direction, and when I get to my desk I see why. There's a newspaper on my desk with a sticky note on it the colour of Lorelei's walls. It says, in Lorelei's handwriting: *I thought we were supposed to be friends—why didn't you tell me?* It seems impossible that a message of anger could be written on this ridiculously happy yellow sticky note.

So while Mr. Gomez is going on at the front about something or another to do with Socrates, I'm trying to get Lorelei's attention. I cough and toss bits of eraser at her, but they don't actually do anything except get stuck in her long, luxurious hair. It's unfair how lovely her hair is. Looking at the back of her head actually makes me happy that I'm in love with her. Otherwise, I would be jealous, but this way I can just admire it instead. For all of history she ignores me. This is not the first time this has happened, and I can't stand it. She gets angry about the smallest things sometimes. Once when I was talking to this guy Andrew, who she kind of thought was cute, she didn't talk to me for two whole days. But I was only asking him about an English assignment; it was nothing. The cold shoulder is too much for me to take. I'm freaking out. What if she never talks to me again? What if I lose her for good this time? I wonder if she felt this panicked when I wasn't talking to her.

When the bell rings she finally looks in my direction. Her eyes look extra green. Almost like Granny-Smith-apple-green, which is totally my favourite kind of apple. She nods toward the door and I jump up, but as I'm following her Mr. Gomez calls out to me.

"Jewel-ie, can I talk to you for a minute?"

What am I supposed to do? Ignore him completely and run away? No. I turn around and he's there, leaning back against his desk, looking casual or maybe fake-casual—I'm not sure.

"Listen, Jewel-ie," he says. "I want you to know that I'm here for you."

"What?" I say. I guess I'm still kind of on the defensive, even though I'm ninety-nine percent sure there was nothing going on the other day. But I still wonder about his intentions with me. And Lorelei.

"I know you're going through a lot right now and it must be really tough," he says. He's practically sitting on his desk. I picture myself crawling up there beside him, touching thighs with him like Lorelei did, his clove breath and gold-rimmed eyes everywhere.

"Lorelei doesn't love you, you know." I had to say it. Just in case he has any ideas in his head. "She just needed help with her school work."

He laughs in this really awkward way, like he can't decide whether to cough or laugh. "That's nice," he says, "but that's not what we're talking about here."

"No?" I ask. I guess I should say that at this point I'm feeling a little bit "uppity," as my dad sometimes likes to call it. I'm mad at Mr. Gomez for stopping me when I was on my way to work things out with Lorelei and I'm mad at Lorelei for making it so we have something to work out in the first place. At the same time, I'm terrified of losing her. On top of all that I can't stop picturing Mom in the park with JC.

In my mind Mom runs off to the cemetery and leaves JC there all alone. What if he gets kidnapped? Or what if she gets ambushed by some reporter and ends up telling the world that she's dead? It will be all my fault for telling her to take JC to the park.

So maybe Mr. Gomez is right. I am going through a lot.

"No. It's not," he says. "I'm worried about you, Jewel-ie. I saw the paper. I can imagine the fire was pretty scary. So I'm here to make it easier for you. Whatever you need or want, you just tell me . . . Is there anything you want to talk about?"

I can't think of a single thing I need or want from Mr. Gomez—expect maybe to be left alone so I can go find Lorelei and sort everything out—and there are obviously a million things I want to talk about, but not with him.

"Perhaps you want to talk about the night of the fire? Sometimes it helps just to get things like that off your chest." Mr. Gomez has this calm, helpful tone to his voice, which is infuriating because it's actually working. It makes me want to pour my heart out. But I wonder if this is all a ploy. Like maybe he's trying to get to me? Does he want *me* to crawl up beside him on his desk? Does he want to seduce *me* with those brown-gold eyes?

"It was bad," I say. "But I really don't need to talk about it."

He furrows his brow and looks so sympathetic it almost makes me believe he really cares.

"How was it bad, Jewel-ie? What happened?"

I lean against a nearby desk and deflate a little. I don't want to, but I just start talking. "There was this doorway. It was so dark and she just vanished into it — like it was swallowing her. I thought she wasn't going to come out." My hands are shaking. I don't want to be having this heart-to-heart with Mr. Gomez, of all people, but the gaping black doorway is etched into my mind and it does feel good to talk about it.

"But she did come out, right?" Mr. Gomez's eyes are so warm and his smile so genuine I can't help but feel better. Maybe I'm just being stupid. Maybe he does just want to help.

"Yes, she did." In my mind I see my mom, bounding from the house, Mr. Wellington safe over her shoulder.

"That's the important part, the part you need to focus on. Can you do that for me?" Mr. Gomez asks.

I nod. "Yeah, thanks." I'm suddenly embarrassed that I fell for his kind-teacher act. I still don't trust that he's not up to something. I take a step toward the door and he watches me go without moving to intercept. "I have to go find Lorelei now."

He doesn't flinch, doesn't bat an eyelash at the sound of her name. "Okay. You just let me know if you need anything," he says.

"Yeah," I reply. Then I run away.

I make a beeline for the bathroom and find Lorelei there, thankfully alone, inspecting her visage and applying her lipstick.

"Hi," I say. I come up behind her and look at her in the mirror. The way we're standing makes it look like we have two heads on one body. Usually I would point something like that out and she would laugh, but this time I don't. "Mr. Gomez stopped me and I only just got away, sorry."

"Yeah," she says.

She doesn't ask what *he* said this time, and it feels unnatural.

"Don't you wanna know what he said?"

"No, I don't really care." She kind of spits a little when she talks. I take a step away from her and lean against the wall, according to bathroom custom. She keeps looking in the mirror and applying her lipstick over and over so her lips are coated in this thick sheen. "So, what the fuck?" she says. "Why didn't you tell me about your mom?"

Her voice feels like a slap. But after the shock of her anger wears off I'm just left feeling annoyed.

"Because I didn't."

"But we're supposed to be best friends," she says. She's still not looking at me, and she keeps pressing her lipstick harder and harder into her lips.

"Yeah, I know we're *supposed to be*." My annoyance comes out in my tone. "Look, Lorelei, I just need a friend right now, okay? It's kind of terrifying having your mom jump into a burning building in front of you, you know? It's not like she was working. She didn't have her gear or anything."

Lorelei turns to me and looks into my eyes. Then her face transforms—her frown melts into a look of deep concern.

"God, I'm sorry, Julie. I don't know what I was thinking," she says. "I'm just stressed about everything with school and I don't want to take it out on you." She moves forward and pulls me into a tight hug. "We *are* best friends, and I don't want to lose that."

I relax in her arms, relieved.

"It's okay," I say.

"Okay, so let's just forget about it then?"

"Yeah, okay. Look, I wasn't joking about helping you. I could tutor you or something."

I can feel her tense in my arms, and when I pull away I can see her blushing. Maybe she doesn't want to admit that she needs help. The Lorelei I have always known has been fearlessly confident. But this Lorelei is different. Like Henry said, sometimes people are different than they seem.

The door whooshes and thumps open and Josie and Carla come in. Here for their daily make-out session before lunch, I guess. We might as well put a sign on the door of that stall with their names on it. I see their wide eyes over Lorelei's shoulder, and Josie giggles and says, "Get a room, lesbos." Then she winks at me, all bold and obvious. I feel my cheeks heat up—I can only imagine they are bright red. Carla grins at me knowingly but doesn't say anything. I don't mind being called a lesbo—even if I'm not fully sure I'm all the way gay—but I guess Lorelei does. She takes a step back from me and tosses her hair in their direction. "Whatever," she says. Then Josie smiles and pulls Carla into their stall, which is apparently the "room" they were referring to.

When the lunch bell rings Lorelei gets up and comes over to my desk. "Maybe we could eat together?" she asks. I want to forget everything that's happened in the past little while because I want at least one thing in my life to be back to normal. So I offer her a bright smile and nod yes.

It's sunny today, with big piles of clouds floating around like cotton balls. As beautiful as it is, I have to work hard to keep pushing thoughts of my mom out of my mind. She's probably fine. She's probably just with JC in the park right now, being normal. Who am I kidding? I'm sure she's at home, in the dining room staring at her hands, thinking nothing, being past tense. I take a deep breath to dispel the panic that image conjures.

I have a tuna sandwich for lunch. It's kind of embarrassing because I know for a fact tuna makes my breath smell bad. It may also have been the reason Lorelei previously thought my breath smelled like pork rinds. So I check my pockets and note with relief that I still have some of those Starbucks mints.

Halfway through lunch Henry comes by. He's back in his shorts and kicking a ball around. He should look normal, but he actually looks totally different from the Henry the other day who was focused on Lorelei and looking all sporty and carefree. It's weird how knowing a person changes their appearance.

"Hi," I say. Obviously, it would be super rude to ignore him completely.

"Hi," he says back. Then he smiles and runs away, his calves going tight and loose and tight and loose.

"He likes you," Lorelei says. She's got a container full of sushi and she's eating it with chopsticks—the height of sophistication.

"No way. We're just friends," I reply. But I think about last night on the swings. How I told him things I could never bring myself to tell Lorelei.

She nods and smiles. She has a bit of nori stuck in her teeth. I tell her and she blushes as she picks it out with the end of her chopstick.

"I heard somewhere that sushi is actually supposed to be a finger food. It wasn't originally intended to be eaten with chopsticks," I say.

"Finger food is unsanitary," she replies, flourishing her chopsticks a bit before she picks up her next roll.

Henry runs by again, legs pumping, smile shining.

Lorelei stands up suddenly. "Can you watch my food? I've got to go to the bathroom. You can have some if you want."

"Yeah," I say. I watch her walk away and go back to my tuna sandwich.

Then all of a sudden here's Henry, ball on hip, leaning against the table.

"How's it going?" he says.

I shrug. "I think she was jealous because I was in the paper." I glance in Lorelei's direction—she's almost made it to the door. "It's kind of terrible. I mean, she didn't even seem to care that my mom could have been hurt." I hate thinking Lorelei could be like that, but I can't just ignore the facts.

Henry shakes his head. "I'm sorry to say it, but it sounds like Lorelei."

"No, honestly, she was just hurt. I'm sure that's all it was," I say, jumping to her defence even if I'm not *actually* sure that's true.

"I don't know," Henry says, shaking his head a little.

"Yeah, me neither," I reply before I can stop myself. I feel bad talking about Lorelei behind her back, but I know Henry won't tell or anything. Plus it's nice to talk to someone who has been close to her too.

"I read the article. It was cool," he says, sliding into the seat across from me at the picnic table. I can feel his leg hairs brushing against my knees.

"Yeah, it's just really surreal, you know, seeing yourself in the newspaper. All this attention on me is kind of stupid though, because I'm not even the hero." I hold up my sandwich in offering to him and he shakes his head no. I don't blame him. The lettuce is wilted and the whole thing is a pinky-grey mush—not appetizing.

"Proximity to celebrity is pretty powerful," he says. He bounces his legs under the table and his hairs tickle my knees. The feeling travels all the way up and all the way down my body, but still I don't move.

"It kind of makes me want to do something brave, you know?"

"What do you want to do?" he asks.

Kiss Lorelei again. Bring my mom back to life. Make Henry's dad talk to him.

"I dunno." I finish my sludgy sandwich then pull out my mints. I take two and give Henry two. He smiles and crunches down on them. Then the sun goes behind a cloud and it suddenly gets cold. I shiver because I'm wearing a T-shirt, and Henry pulls off his soccer sweatshirt and tosses it at me.

"No, it's okay." I try to hand it back.

But he flips his hand and grins. "No worries, just one friend to another."

I put it on. Thankfully, it doesn't smell like cologne, but it does smell like boy. I don't know how else to describe it: it's just boyish. Like kind of sweaty and kind of deodoranty and something else too. A good smell.

"So I was thinking about your dad," I say. Henry looks down at his hands in this pained way that reminds me of Mom at the dining-room table. Maybe looking down at your hands is an international sign for distress.

"Really, he just needs time," Henry says.

"I know but, like, in the meantime maybe you could hire someone. . . a maid or something?"

He shrugs like he really doesn't want to be talking about this and looks back up at me. The sun comes back out right then as if it's on cue. His eyes go bright blue. It almost looks like they're a part of the sky.

"I'm sorry," I say. I don't want him to think I'm butting into his life.

"No, it's a good idea," he says.

"Hey, lovebirds, what's the word?" Lorelei says, coming up behind me and slipping back into her seat.

Henry laughs. "We're not lovebirds," he says.

"We were just talking about Iran," I say. "I was telling him about all the stuff we were debating in UN, the nukes and everything." It feels strange to lie to Lorelei like that—it was too quick, too easy.

She rolls her eyes and grins. "So, geeking out together basically? What a party."

Henry stands up and grabs his ball from the table. "Well, I guess I'll leave you two alone now."

I struggle to take off the sweatshirt but he waves his hand at me again. "Keep it. I'll get it later." Then he runs off.

"I told you he likes you. Maybe it's even love," Lorelei says, fishing out a big piece of sushi and sticking all of it into her mouth.

"Whatever. He can like whoever he wants, I don't care."

Lorelei's laugh is muffled by raw fish and rice.

After lunch it's gym. Mrs. Singh pulls me out of the dodge ball game and into her little office. It's cramped with gym supplies and smells like a locker room. I can't say I'm unhappy to have been pulled out of class though, because dodge ball is a ludicrous and barbaric game that has no place in schools—or anywhere else in life, for that matter. It's at this point that I remember

Mrs. Singh is doubling as the guidance counsellor, since layoffs this year mean the actual counsellor, Miss Penhale, is gone.

"I think we should talk about everything that's been happening," Mrs. Singh says. She talks in a really nice sort of way, with a lilting accent. I hunker down in my chair and Henry's sweatshirt slips up. It's a bit too big for me, and now I'm wondering why I didn't take it off for gym.

"What do you want to talk about?" I ask.

"How is everything at home?"

"Fine."

"It can't be easy, all the attention all of a sudden," Mrs. Singh says.

"It's okay—a bit awkward, I guess. Mostly just people being extra nice to me."

A ball flies at the door and hits it with such a loud bang it's almost painful.

"They should really give you a wooden door," I say.

She laughs and leans back in her chair, looking more relaxed than I've ever seen her. "They should give me a lot of things. A real office, for example," she says.

"This is a little . . . cramped."

"How diplomatic of you, Julie. Listen, I want you to know you can talk to me. About anything. That's what I'm here for, and I don't want you to feel like you're alone in all of this."

I nod. She's so nice and calm and soft that for a minute I wish I could just dive right into her arms and whisper all of my secrets in her ear. She would at least be a better person to talk to than Mr. Gomez. Then another ball hits the door and snaps me out of it.

"Actually, I wanted to ask you if I could go study. I kind of fell behind in my school work with everything that's going on, and I just want to get a few things done." The truth is I've been falling steadily behind in school since Mom started acting weird. I flunked a math test the other day for the first time in forever.

"Of course, Julie, that is completely understandable," Mrs. Singh says.

I stand up and almost knock over a big pile of mats in the process. Mrs. Singh tells me not to worry about it and sends me out to the yard with my school work. I sit for a while and try not to think about Mom and JC in the park. I try hard to focus on my math textbook, but all the numbers and lines keep blurring together. So instead of working, I just fold myself up into Henry's sweatshirt and nap until the bell rings and everyone emerges from gym all sweaty and covered in red splotches from not dodging the ball.

• • •

After school Lorelei and I meet up to walk to her house for the dreaded funeral.

"So, I can't believe all that stuff really happened, with the fire and everything," she says as we make our way out into the sunshine.

I push the image of the dark doorway out of my mind. "Yeah, it was pretty cool, I guess, but it was mostly just horrible."

She grabs onto my hand and smiles. "It seems more exciting than scary. I bet I would have rescued that old guy too, like your mom did."

I'm positive that's not true.

"Well, you're braver than me," I reply, "because all I did was watch and freak out instead of trying to help."

Lorelei squeezes my hand, but she doesn't reply. Walking hand in hand with her should feel both normal and exciting, but something has changed ever since I saw her with Mr. Gomez.

When we get to her house we head to her room to change. It reminds me of the night we kissed when we were getting ready for the party. This time there's no kissing though, just a small feeling of dread building in my stomach. Lorelei slips into a conservative black dress, and she lends me black pants and a black top. I try not to think about the funeral. I don't want to go to a place where everything is past tense.

The church isn't far so we walk there. It's old and musty and creaky like my house, so it feels familiar. We're there early, and as we watch Pastor Greenwood set up, I notice how beautiful it is: there are these rainbow stained glass windows, and when the sun shines through them the rainbowness falls onto the floor.

Lorelei shows me around. She looks proud that she knows all the secrets of the place, like the drawer where the wine/blood of Christ is kept and the hidden entrance to a secret room behind the altar. The secret room is a flower room, literally full of flowers and vases and those green squishy blocks that you stick flower stems into to make them stand up properly. It smells so good in there that we hang around for a bit. I walk around the room naming all the different types of flowers I can.

"Hyacinth, rose, obviously, chrysanthemum, baby's breath, violet, black-eyed Susan, daffodil, forget-me-not, birds of paradise . . . "

Lorelei looks impressed and smells each one after I've named it, like she's confirming their names with her nose. "I'm going to have birds of paradise at my wedding," she says, taking one out of a vase and arranging it in her hair. "Most people have roses or something boring, but I want mine to be exotic."

I imagine her walking down the aisle holding a bouquet of birds of paradise, and smiling at me as I wait for her at the altar. I wonder if her father would agree to marry us. Then suddenly another image pops into my mind. It's me walking down the aisle toward Henry.

"Nice choice," I say quickly, hoping she doesn't notice the red heat in my cheeks. "I read somewhere that the bird of paradise symbolizes magnificence."

Lorelei laughs. "Perfect."

The image of Henry fades as Lorelei's smile fills my vision.

During the funeral we sit in the back row, and it is indeed an open casket. I can't stop staring at the coffin lid and imagining it opening and closing like a mouth. Lorelei and I are wedged in beside one another on the stiff wooden pew. It's so uncomfortable it makes me really glad I'm not religious. I wouldn't want to have to sit here every Sunday for services and listen to Pastor Greenwood while my butt hurt and my legs fell asleep.

Pastor Greenwood makes a really nice but too-long speech about the lady in the casket and family and life and walking through the valley of the shadow of death. I'm pretty overwhelmed by how much he talks about God too, given the funeral isn't for God.

"In all my conversations with God," Pastor Greenwood says, "I have been assured of Maureen's place in heaven, of her everlasting serenity and benevolent watchfulness from above. She was a wonderful woman, and she will find all that wonder returned to her three-fold in the sweet embrace of eternity. She will walk forever in God's grace." There's a shifting in the crowd as the pastor bows his head and a cacophony of sniffling echoes off the ceiling. I wonder if Maureen really *was* a wonderful person.

Next come the speeches from friends and family, and it's about midway through the daughter's speech when she starts to cry and I start to laugh. I don't mean to, but the giggle rises up from my stomach and bubbles out of my mouth. Lorelei looks at me with wide eyes, and some people in front of us shift in their seats like they're getting ready to turn around and glare at me. I try to tamp it down but the laughter keeps coming up, up, up through my mouth and out into the open air. Maureen's daughter is crying even harder now, but I still can't stop laughing. The giggles are coming out even louder. Lorelei jabs me with her elbow and I fall out of my seat into the aisle. Gasping, I run outside.

Out in the sunshine I take massive gulps of air. I just keep gulping and gulping and laughing and laughing until tears are streaming down my face and I'm laughing in this horribly painful way that I can't stop even though I want to more than anything. Then Lorelei comes out and frowns at me with her hand on her hip and I'm just doubled over cracking up until I finally settle down.

"What was that?" Lorelei asks.

Would I call Lorelei *wonderful* if I had to give her eulogy?

"I don't know," I reply as I sit down on the church steps, exhausted.

"Well, now we can't get the food because there's no way we can go back in there," she says.

"Sorry," I reply, still struggling for breath. "It just happened. I don't know what's wrong with me."

She sighs and sits down beside me. Then pats my leg like it's a dog. "It's okay. You're new to this. It was probably just nerves. You'll do better next time."

I don't want to tell her there won't be a next time, that I hate this church and its *wonderful* dusty rainbows, so I just nod and stay quiet.

We leave before the funeral is over because Lorelei is positive we'll get dirty looks. On the way home we stop by 7-Eleven so I can buy her an I'm-sorry pack of licorice. When we get home there's a note on the counter in perfect cursive from Mrs. Greenwood. It says she's gone out to her book club and there are sandwiches in the fridge in case we didn't have enough to eat at the funeral. It's all dips and loops and she's dotted her *i*'s with tiny perfect circles.

We sit at the kitchen counter and eat ham-and-cheese sandwiches. We bite both ends of our licorice to make the pieces into straws and drink some orange juice.

"Where do you think she's going?" I ask. "The dead lady, Maureen, I mean."

"The graveyard," Lorelei replies.

"I know *that*," I say, "but I mean after that."

"I don't know. Heaven, I guess?" she says.

"I guess." I try to imagine my mom in heaven, eating marshmallows and flying around or whatever people do in heaven. But all I can see is her body lying terribly still under the bedsheet on the coffee table. I try to replace that image with one of her flying through the air toward the burning house. That is how I want to see her, remember her. A superhero. "It's just I can't see it, you know? Like, what does it even mean to go to heaven? It seems so convenient."

"It is," Lorelei says. She pauses to chew and swallow a bite of her sandwich. "Look, it's very convenient, and that's why people like it, that's why *I* like it. It's nicer than the alternative, than nothing, right?" She speaks quickly, like she doesn't want to be saying the words. Like she's scared of them.

"What does heaven look like to you?" I ask.

Lorelei looks up, like she's trying to see through the ceiling into the sky above. "I try not to think about it too much. It's like one of those Impressionist paintings that looks good from far away, but up close it just falls apart."

"Oh," I reply.

She looks over at me and her expression softens. "But I guess it's more like a feeling than anything, that everything will be okay."

"That's how I feel when I'm with you," I say. "You're so self-assured that I always feel like everything is going to be fine when you're around." I blush as the words pour out and I look down at the counter when I realize what I've said.

She smiles and leans over to catch my gaze. "That's a gorgeous thing to say, dahling."

"I mean it."

"I love the way you think about things, Julie. I feel smarter when you're around, like maybe I could absorb some of your brains by osmosis."

I laugh and we grin at each other. And for a minute it's not about kissing her, or telling her I'm in love with her. It's just about us being friends. Simple.

11.

I had my first school dance when I was eleven. This guy named Carlo asked me to go with him and I said yes, even though I really wanted to go with Lorelei. When I came home that day I cried and told my mom everything. She listened and smiled and said, "Julie, sweetie, you have to be who you are. If you want to go to the dance with Lorelei, tell Carlo no and ask her instead." I told Carlo no but I couldn't bring myself to ask Lorelei. My mom was right, but I didn't always listen to her.

A week later and we're all back on the stage. We're drinking juice and eating cookies and Lorelei is going on about decor and asking us if we've finished our projects. Nima and Gwen have joined the committee too, which is kind of awkward because it's obviously just to get closer to me. They spend more time trying to strike up a conversation with me than paying attention to Lorelei. Everyone just tries to ignore them though, myself included.

Lorelei is updating everyone about the plans and she has a copy of my poster, which is pretty cool, if I do say so myself. Maybe if Lorelei becomes an event planner I can be her graphic designer. The poster's got a shadow lady half in lingerie and half in a cutesy dress and the words are artfully arranged around her. I was actually surprised it got approved, given the provocative nature of the picture and the uptightness of the principal.

"So the dance is next Friday and we're going to need to figure out the booze situation," Lorelei says. She whispers the word *booze* because Mrs. Singh is in her office with the door open. She's probably not actually paying attention, but who knows. "I think we'll have to recruit someone to guard the punch bowl. It's gotta be someone the teachers won't want to go near. How about Sheila?"

I don't think this is a good idea. The spiked punch is bad enough. If we get caught, Lorelei will for sure get sent away to boarding school. And now we're involving Sheila? This has trouble written all over it.

"Who's gonna ask her?" I say. But what I want to say is, Wow, is this ever a dumb idea.

Lorelei grins. "I will. It's perfect, if you think about it. I mean, no one is even going to go near the table with her standing guard."

"*I* won't even want to go near the table," Nima says, and everyone laughs nervously.

"Why would she agree to this, anyway?" I ask. I'm trying to find a way out of this without stomping all over Lorelei's excitement.

"Free booze, obviously," Lorelei whispers.

I look around at the group. Everyone just shrugs.

"As long as she promises to behave," Ed Simpson says, eyes glued to his phone, as usual.

"Of course," Lorelei replies, as if she alone has the power to make Sheila behave. "Anyway, moving on," she continues. "We have the decor budget locked down and I'll be picking up the booze this weekend." Again she whispers the word *booze*. "So we should be all set. Thanks for coming, everyone, and pitching in. I think this is going to be the best dance ever!" I'm still not convinced this booze thing is a good idea, but Lorelei is so sure I decide to drop it. Maybe she really has found her calling as a party planner and everything will be just fine.

I wait for Lorelei on the front steps while she runs to her locker to grab her stuff. I'm happy to report that the spring is pretty summer-like today, so the sun is nice and hot. There's a soccer game in the field and I watch it for a bit. I spot Henry with the ball, running and kicking. He looks so happy out there, like he did on the swings last week. And again I find myself thinking he might be kind of cute.

Lorelei interrupts my thoughts when she bounds out the front doors and almost trips over me. She giggles and says sorry, then she grabs my hand and we walk toward my house. And I'd like to say that with Lorelei's hand in mine all thoughts of Henry quickly vanish, but they don't. He lingers in the back of my mind as we walk.

"So where are you gonna get the alcohol?" I ask.

"Jamal's brother Sammy is going to buy it for us—you know, the guy who had the party?" She says this very casually, like it's not a big deal. But I didn't realize that Lorelei was on a first-name basis with Jamal's brother—never mind a buying-booze basis. The thought makes me instinctively jealous. I'm still not one hundred percent sure how I feel about Lorelei these days, but my love for her is habitual.

"Oh, is that why you went upstairs that night?" I ask, equally casual. That party feels like it was a million years ago.

"Yeah, and the upstairs party was *way* cooler." She laughs and tosses her hair. The ends of it hit my face and leave me with the lingering scent of her shampoo. She doesn't say that I should have come upstairs too. She doesn't even try to say she was just going upstairs to use the bathroom, like she told me that night. She just leaves it at that, an open-ended mystery.

"Cool," I say.

"So listen. I'm gonna need you to take the booze and keep it at your house, okay?" Lorelei says, her voice a little too relaxed. She always sounds this way when she's asking for a favour.

"What? Why?"

"Because if I get caught it's off to boarding school."

"I guess," I say. "But what about my parents?" I'm trying to get out of it, because I didn't even like the idea of booze in the punch in the first place, but we both know my parents would definitely be more lenient, especially with my mom being so out of it.

"What would happen?" she says sweetly. "You'd get grounded. It's not nearly as bad as boarding school." This isn't the first time she's gotten me to do something I don't want to do. Like in grade eight when she convinced me to let her copy off my math exam, and I did it because of that sweet tone in her voice. Luckily, we never got caught.

"I guess."

She giggles. "I knew you'd be up for it, Julie."

I'm not up for it at all, but what else can I do? I don't have the guts to say no. I never have the guts to say no to her.

"So it's settled then. Perfect. Anyway," Lorelei continues, "what are you going to wear to the dance? You can borrow whatever—maybe my red dress?"

She's already told me that the red dress is Henry's favourite, but I don't want to wear Henry's favourite—do I?

"What do you think I should wear?" I ask.

"Hmmm . . . probably the red." She looks off into the distance like she's imagining me in the dress. The way the sun is falling makes her eyes look grey.

"Okay, sure, I guess."

She grins at me brightly.

"Do you want to come over for dinner?" I ask.

"No, I've got to get home," she says. "Thanks though."

"Well, do you want to hang out this weekend?" We've arrived at my house already. I lean against the door but don't make a move to go inside. Partly because I want to extend my time with her, but mostly because I don't want to deal with my mom.

"I've got, like, so much homework this weekend. I've been slacking. Plus I've got to hook up with Sammy."

The way she says it makes it sound like she's going to *actually* hook up with him. But that's not what she means—is it?

"But I'll see you for a minute or two at least, after I meet up with Sammy." She winks at me conspiratorially.

I just shrug and smile. I don't want to beg to hang out with her. "Okay."

"Sorry." She leans in and kisses me on the cheek and I feel a small shiver spread out from the point of contact. My mind is unclear on my feelings, but obviously my body isn't.

"Let me know if you need help with, you know, your homework," I say quietly.

She flushes and flashes me a quick grin. "Thanks." I watch her walk away until she rounds the corner. Then I keep watching for a bit longer before I head inside.

I avoid the dining room completely because I don't want to see my mom in there, sitting alone in the thin light, all quiet and pale. Once I get into my room I slip on Henry's sweatshirt and sit down on my bed. I think about texting him, but he's probably still playing soccer, so I try to focus on homework instead. There are a couple of big exams coming up, and I have a few final projects in the works. I can't let my grades slip even more than they currently have.

The JC alarm goes off again tonight. I hear the creak of Mom on the floorboards so I stumble out of bed. It is possible she just wants to calm JC with a ride, but I'm not taking any chances that she won't run off into the cemetery all night and leave JC alone in the car.

We cruise down the quiet streets and I press my head against the window. I'm just about ready to fall asleep when we pass the park and I see a single, sad shape sitting on the swing.

"Stop, Mom, stop," I say. She pulls over to the side of the road in front of the park. I get out and run toward the swing. The sad shape perks up a bit and says, "Julie?"

It's definitely Henry, and he definitely looks like something is weighing him down. His shoulders are so stooped it looks painful.

"I was hoping you'd come."

"It's one in the morning, Henry."

"I've been here for a while," he replies.

"You should have texted."

He shrugs and I step closer.

"I forgot my phone," he says.

"Are you okay?" I ask, even though it seems like a dumb question. Why would he be out here so late if he was okay?

"Nice sweatshirt," he replies.

"Do you want it?" He looks cold, all hunched over in his T-shirt on the swing.

"Naw, it looks better on you."

That makes me smile even though I kind of think I should force the sweatshirt on him: he looks pretty pathetic, and I don't want to be responsible for him freezing to death. Then I remember Mom is waiting in the car.

"Do you want to come with me?" I ask.

He shrugs. "Where you going?"

"Does it matter?" I look around at the obvious lack of better offers.

He slips off the swing and comes toward me.

"So what happened?" I ask.

"Absolutely nothing," he says. "That's the problem." I stick him in the back of the car with JC and we keep driving. Henry seems happy with the silence and so am I. Obviously Mom is too.

"I like car rides," Henry says at one point.

"Me too," I reply.

Henry doesn't comment when we pull through the gates of Mount Pleasant Cemetery and creep along the little graveyard roads toward Grandpa James's final resting place. He doesn't comment when we stop and sit in silence. Or when Mom stares out the window with a terrible, ghoulish longing at all the stones lined up like silver teeth in the starlight. He doesn't say a word when we get out of the car and leave JC behind. Or when we pass over all the people I've passed so many times before. He doesn't speak when we stop at Grandpa James's grave, where the flowers are wilted and rotten because no one has thought to change them.

Then Mom kneels for a long time. She's looking at the gravestone like she's forgotten how to read and is trying really hard to remember. I glance over at Henry. He looks tired and melancholy and sweet. He's wearing this solemn expression that seems like it's probably reserved for graveside visits and funerals and other occasions where you're not supposed to smile. I sidle up to him and take his hand. It's really warm.

"That's my Grandpa James," I whisper, my voice catching a little in my throat. "He raised my mom all by himself and she misses him all the time."

Henry bows his head a little like he's acknowledging me and Grandpa James and Mom all in one gesture. I think it's a nice thing to do, so I squeeze his hand and we stand silently for a bit while Mom kneels there, a thin line of sadness on the grass. Then she puts her hands down on the earth. My chest gets tight and a lump forms in my throat as she slides down onto the ground and rolls onto her back.

"No, Mom," I whisper. "What are you doing?"

"I'm playing a game," she says quietly. "It's called Rest in Peace. You have to bury me and say all the nice things about me you can think of."

I drop to my knees beside her, my skin feeling tight around my bones.

"Please get up, Mom. We can play, but you have to get up."

She shakes her head and closes her eyes. My heart thunks hard in my chest. I didn't want Henry to see this, and she shouldn't either, but I guess she's way beyond caring. I look up at Henry. He's looking down at me, brow creased into an oversized frown.

"This is a game we play," I say. "She's never done this part before though. She wants us to bury her."

And Henry doesn't say a word. He just kneels down on the ground and picks up a handful of dead leaves. Then he puts them on her stomach like he's played this game a million times before. And of course this makes me cry. I cry quietly in the dark while Henry does all of the burying and even adds the flowers. Then I say the past-tense part because he doesn't really know my mom that well so it wouldn't be fair.

"Here lies a great hero," I say through my tears, "a wonderful mom and a good firefighter. A woman who made excellent macaroni and taught me many things." I can't go on anymore. The word *wonderful* tastes bitter on my tongue and I'm breathing in these great, huge gulps. Every part of me is sore. All I can do is wrap my arms around myself in Henry's sweatshirt and sob. Then I realize Henry's sweatshirt can't really compare to Henry himself, so I turn to him. He lets me hold him and cry onto his shoulder. I cry so much I make his shirt wet, which probably makes him even colder, but he doesn't seem to care.

After what feels like an hour we both start to shiver in each other's arms. This has gone on long enough. I lean down over my mom and say, "Enough now, Mom. It's time to go."

But she doesn't move.

"Come on, Mom, let's go," I say, louder this time.

Again, no movement beneath the grass and leaves and wilted flowers. Her eyes are open now, but she doesn't seem to see me leaning over her. She's just staring straight up into the sky.

So now I'm down on my knees sweeping all the earth off my mom's thin body, and there's so much on there it scares me. Soon Henry is beside me and we're both sweeping and sweeping until finally she's clear of debris, but she still doesn't move. I put my head on her chest and I hear a heartbeat. I feel the slight push and pull of her breath. I have no idea why she won't move.

"Mom, come on," I say. "Game over, okay?"

Henry puts his hands on her shoulders and shakes her lightly. "Mrs. Nolan?" Still nothing. Now I'm starting to panic. I get up and pace around.

"So what? We're stuck in the graveyard now? This can't be happening," I say.

"We could carry her," Henry suggests.

"To the car? But who's gonna drive?"

"I can," he says.

What other choice do we have?

We carry Mom, who is way too light, through the cemetery like a couple of grave robbers. Making our way across the graves and into the car, we tuck her into the back seat, and JC moans a little in his sleep as we shut the door. Then Henry buckles into the driver's seat. He eases us along the starlit roads of the cemetery and back to the main road. He drives carefully all the way home. We carry Mom in first and lay her down on the couch. She continues to stare upward like she never actually left the graveyard and is still lying on the cold, damp ground looking up at the stars. We bring JC in next and tuck him into his basket. Then without discussion we go to my room and crawl into bed. I think about erecting a pillow wall between us, but I'm too cold and tired and scared and sad to do anything. So I let Henry envelop me beneath the covers and I listen to his breath in my ear until we both fall into a deep, dark sleep.

12.

Lorelei got her first official boyfriend when I was twelve. I was destroyed. I came home from school everyday with a stomach ache and my mom would leave work early to sit with me. She would give me hot water bottles and we would watch TV, whatever shows I wanted. She tried to take me to the doctor but I said no. Eventually I told her everything. That's how it was with Mom; no matter how much I wanted to keep my secrets, I would always spill my guts to her in the end. She wrapped her arms around me and kissed my head and said, "Love can suck sometimes, Julie, but it's best to be honest. Tell her how you feel." I wish I could have been as brave as my mom wanted me to be.

When I wake up in bed with another person I expect it to be Lorelei. But when I roll over, I see Henry staring at me. And for a second I get trapped in his blue, blue gaze. So I look hard, because I want to catch a glimpse of his soul.

"What are you doing?" he asks.

I blush because I'm not even sure I believe in souls. But he already knows enough about me at this point that it seems stupid to be embarrassed.

"I'm trying to see your soul. I kind of thought you were soulless before, but I've changed my mind now—total three-sixty."

He laughs and props his head up on his hand, elbow bent, so he's looking down at me. "Thanks, I guess, but wouldn't it be a one-eighty?"

"Why?" I mirror his posture. Now I'm at least an inch closer to his face.

"Well, three-sixty would take you back to where you started, wouldn't it? And a one-eighty would take you somewhere new."

"Yeah, but if you think about it a different way, a three-sixty would take me all the way to a new opinion, whereas a one-eighty would take me only halfway."

"Oh, right. I guess if you think about it that way . . . "

"It's all metaphorical anyway though, so you could be right too."

"No, I like yours better—fresh start, new circle," he says. Then he closes his eyes and the room gets darker because the sun has passed behind a cloud. When he opens his eyes again they look concerned. "What's wrong with her, Julie?" he asks.

I sit up on the bed and cross my legs. I can kind of smell his breath from here and it's surprisingly sweet, mixed with regular old morning breath, of course, which everybody has—even Lorelei.

"I don't know," I say.

"How long have you been . . . playing that game?" Henry asks. The way he says *game* makes it sound like the least fun thing anyone has ever done.

"A couple weeks. She's going to a shrink today," I say. I feel bad telling Henry that, but if Mom was in the right headspace she'd probably tell him herself. She's pretty open about that kind of stuff: once at dinner she told me and Lorelei all about her ob-gyn appointment, which was pretty gross and graphic, but she thought it would be good for us to know what we were in for as adults.

"I went to therapy once," Henry says.

"Really? How was it? I heard you just have to talk about yourself a lot."

He shrugs and sits up too, so we are face to face again. "It was through the school, after my mom died. They thought I would want to talk to someone."

"Did it help? I mean, did you talk about your dad?"

He shakes his head. "I mostly just talked about my memories of my mom." He looks down at his hands, weaving his fingers together like a braid. "It was kind of nice, you know, to have someone give a crap about me, listen to me and talk to me. It helped with the silent treatment I was getting at home."

I don't know what to say.

"Sorry," he says.

"What for?" I play with the cuff of my sweater, his sweater, for something to do.

"I don't want to be all whiny and putting my issues on you. That's lame."

"Don't be ridiculous. You helped me carry my mom to the car last night and drove us home, so let's call it even, okay?"

"Okay." He smiles and leans forward and our faces are so close I'm pretty sure he's about to kiss me. I jump out of bed quickly.

"What's wrong?" he says. He looks shocked at my quick exit.

"Nothing, I'm just really hungry," I say.

I'm suddenly really self-conscious that I'm still wearing his sweatshirt. I gave Henry some of my clothes last night from my serious boy phase, when I insisted my parents buy me stuff two sizes too big. The sweatpants and T-shirt fit him perfectly—they even look pretty good. "Come on," I say, and make a beeline for the door.

When we get downstairs JC is sleeping in his basket, hugging his dirt- and slobber-covered donkey.

Mom is nowhere to be found. I'm surprised at first, but then I realize this is actually a good thing because it means whatever deal Dad made with her to get her to go to the shrink actually worked. Saturday morning is shrink morning. I can't believe she made it out the door by herself after last night, but maybe she actually got some sleep. I would have preferred she didn't leave JC down here on his own, but as Dad always says: beggars can't be choosers. At least JC has a clean diaper and a half-empty bottle sitting beside his basket.

My stomach growls and Henry's does too. Then we both laugh and stomach growl in tandem. I tell him to go hang out in the living room and I'll make us some breakfast. The truth is I'm not a master chef. It's pathetic, but Mom usually cooks for me in the morning and makes my lunches and dinners and stuff. So I just root around in the fridge for some fruit and yogurt. Then instead, in a fit of inspiration, I decide to make pancakes from a box I find in the cupboard. It's a bit of a disaster, which ends with me climbing up onto a chair and taking down the fire alarm, then running into the dining room to quiet down JC, who's freaking out about the alarm. But I don't give up—I should be able to make something as simple as stupid pancakes.

I'm standing by the stove flipping the dumb, clumpy things when I hear a creak. I turn around to see Henry in the door with JC in his arms, smiling over at me.

"Do you know how to cook?" I ask.

"Yup," he says.

Then he holds up JC and we do a trade, spatula for baby. Before long we're eating golden pancakes with fruit and maple syrup at the dining-room table and JC is sleeping in his basket. I feel really proud of both of us.

"We're like an old married couple," I say, mouth full of pancake.

"I thought you were gay," he replies, his blue eyes watching me closely from across the table.

"I'm not sure I'm fully gay, but at least a little," I say.

"What's that like?" he asks.

"It's like I'm attracted to girls—well, specifically Lorelei. I want to kiss her and be together with her all the time." At least I *wanted* that.

"I know what that's like—with girls, I mean, not just Lorelei."

"Do you think someone can really be bisexual? I mean, that girl Carmen Ellis claims she is, but everyone thinks she just says it to be cool."

He thinks about it for a minute, swirling his syrup with his fork. "Yeah, well, my uncle's best friend is bi—there's a couple of bi kids on *Degrassi* too."

"You watch *Degrassi*?" I ask. That's the kind of show I would never get away with watching when my mom was normal. She's big on educational viewing, not so much with the teen drama.

"Yeah." He shrugs and looks down at his plate, embarrassed.

"It's just funny. I never thought you were the type of person to watch that," I say.

"Well, what kind of person did you think I was?" he asks.

Now it's my turn to look at my plate. "I don't know. I mean, I didn't really think about you that much before except when I was hating you because you were dating Lorelei."

He laughs. "Well, I watch all kinds of shows, especially with no one to stop me."

I smile at him and shove a big forkful of pancake in my mouth.

"Anyway, I think you can like guys and girls. It's just about who you connect with, you know?" he says. "Like, who you want to talk to and tell stuff to and spend time with."

"And who you want to kiss?" I ask.

"Yeah, that too."

There's a bit of an awkward moment where I think about Lorelei's lipsticked lips and Henry thinks about hopefully not me.

Our silence is broken by the phone ringing. I run to pick it up. I think it's probably Dad calling to check in, and I feel kind of bad because he would probably frown on me having Henry here overnight—but what's one more secret, right?

"Hello?"

"Hi, I'm looking for Mrs. Nolan. Is she in?" It's not Dad. It's a woman and she sounds super professional.

"Can I ask who's calling?"

"Yes, this is Dr. Phillips's office." Dr. Phillips. The shrink. I close my eyes and take a deep breath, my fingers tingling with tension.

"My mom is with Dr. Phillips right now," I say quietly.

"That's what I'm calling about, actually. She missed her appointment, so I wanted to reschedule." I pace through the kitchen like my feet are on fire. If she's not with the shrink, where is she? Back in the graveyard?

"Well, she's not home right now, but I can get her to call in and reschedule, okay?"

"Great, thanks."

"Bye," I say too quickly.

Then I hang up and immediately dial Mom's cell. It goes straight to voicemail. I hang up and run into the dining room. Frantic. My face feels hot and my fingers are definitely tingling in that panicky way that I hate.

Henry stands up. "What is it?"

"Mom's not at the doctor and she's not picking up her phone."

"What should we do?"

I think about calling the police, about calling Dad. But then I would have to tell him the whole story and I promised Mom I would keep her secret. I promised.

"I don't know but we have to do something. Maybe we should go look for her at the graveyard. We could take the subway . . . "

My talking-way-too-fast rant is cut short when the front door opens and my mom walks in. She stands in the hall and looks in on us in the dining room. I think I almost see a smile on her face, but it might just be a memory. I run over and grab her by the shoulders.

"This isn't fair! You were supposed to be at the doctor!" I shake her a little and her head bobs back and forth like a bobblehead. She blinks at me, and for a second a look of recognition passes through her eyes.

"I forgot," she says simply.

"No, that's not good enough. You have to make a new appointment, okay? Where were you?"

"Driving," she says.

I shake my head. The panic is draining from my body, but not fast enough. I still feel like my skin is on fire and I just ran a marathon.

Henry is standing behind me, looking like he wants

to do something to help. I flap my hand at him and he goes to sit back down.

"Okay, Mom," I say. "You can't do that again, all right? If you don't go to your appointments I am going to have to tell Dad so he can take you."

She frowns at me and shakes her head. "Maxwell is busy."

"I know he's busy, but you have to cut me some slack. You have to help me out, okay?"

"Okay," she says.

But I'm not convinced.

"Okay. Do you want some pancakes? Henry made them; he's a really good cook."

"No," she says. She's holding onto the frame of the entrance to the dining room and her knuckles are white from the effort.

"Well, maybe you can watch some TV while I finish breakfast?"

I help her take off her coat then guide her to the couch and sit her down. I wrap a blanket around her knees because her hands are so cold it's scary.

"How about we cut your hair today, before Dad gets home?" I say.

Mom's hair is all wiry and frayed from the fire. It's so frazzled I can't look at it without thinking of embers and burning and smoke. She's always cut my hair for me, so I figure it's time to return the favour.

"Max is coming back tomorrow," Mom says. She's talking slow, like a little kid who doesn't really know how to speak that well. Things are definitely going downhill with her. I have to make sure she gets to therapy.

"Yeah," I reply.

I leave Mom by the TV and go back to Henry. He's finished his food but is waiting politely for me to come back and finish mine, but I'm not hungry anymore.

"Do you want to stay over tonight too? My Dad's not getting back until tomorrow," I say.

"Are you sure it's okay?" he asks.

"Well, I'm the adult around here right now, and I say yes, so yes."

"I'm not gonna argue with an adult then."

We both laugh, but mine comes out a little sad and pathetic because I'm still so stressed.

"Have you told your dad about all this?" Henry asks, looking down at his empty plate and shifting a withered, gross-looking grape around with his fork.

"Mom told me not to. Dad's so tired and stressed all the time. It's pretty tense right now."

"This is a lot to take on by yourself," he says, looking me straight in the eye.

"I know. But I'm not some little kid. I can handle it."

"I didn't mean . . . "

"I know, sorry." I guess it came out kind of defensive. "It's a lot, but I want to take care of her, you know?"

"Yeah." He sounds like he really does know.

"Anyway, I'm going to cut my mom's hair after breakfast," I say, brightly.

"Can't you just take her to a hairdresser?" Henry asks.

"I want to do it myself. She always does it for me — it's like a ritual or something. Do you go to church?"

He looks over at me and shakes his head. "Nope."

JC is fussing in his basket so I grab him and cradle him in my arms. I rock him back and forth until he calms down. "I went to a place called the Casket Depot the other day and it looked like a cathedral. So I call it the Casket Cathedral now. There was this woman all in purple named Violet. Mom lay down in a coffin and the whole thing was pretty spiritual. More spiritual than going to Lorelei's dad's church even."

"Church is overrated," Henry says. "People make a big deal out of it but I don't get it, personally."

"Me neither. We went to a funeral at Lorelei's dad's church and I just started laughing. I couldn't stop, and we had to leave. Lorelei was pissed because it meant we couldn't get the food all the old ladies had made," I say. It's not like I'm saying all this stuff to fill an awkward silence or anything. With Henry I don't feel any awkwardness in the silences. I'm saying it because I want to tell him, because it seems like something he would get, or at least not judge.

"I laughed at my mom's funeral," he says.

"Oh, crap," I reply.

"Yeah."

"Can I ask you something?"

"Shoot."

"Did you give her eulogy?"

Henry sighs. "Yeah, I said some garbage about how great she was and all the stuff she did for me."

"Did you say she was wonderful?" I ask. I shift JC around because his head is resting on my arm and making it fall asleep.

"I don't know, why?"

I shrug. "That's why I laughed at the funeral. I was thinking about how they called the dead woman wonderful and how I do that too when I say my mom's eulogy. I was thinking about how shallow it is. I can't stand that I can never think of anything more to say about my mom."

"I'm not sure there are any words that say what we really mean, are there?" Henry asks. "There are no words I could think of to say how much I loved my mom, how much I miss her. How could words sum that up? Everything she gave me—I don't think the words we use are shallow, they're just . . . inadequate."

It's hard to breathe because I'm so sad for Henry and for myself. I don't want to look at him, but I don't want to not look at him. I have no idea what to say, so

I put my hand down on the table between us, palm up, and wait until his hand falls into mine. Then I squeeze. I actually squeeze his hand so tight that I accidentally squeeze JC too, and he shifts like a little worm squirming around. I'm suddenly all filled up with love and sadness.

"I'm so sorry," I say.

"It's okay," Henry replies.

But I'm not sure that it is.

After breakfast Henry hangs out on the couch while I cut my mom's hair. She wears an old shirt, and chunks of seared hair float to the ground like fall leaves. She sits really still. Even though I have no idea what I'm doing, it looks pretty good when I'm done. I show her in the mirror and she definitely smiles—it's not just a memory.

"Looking good," I say.

"You have a way with hair," she replies. That makes me so happy because we usually have the same conversation, but opposite, when she cuts my hair.

After I sweep up, Mom changes her shirt and I make her call the shrink to schedule a new appointment. I listen while she does it and hope beyond hope that this time she'll go. If she actually goes to the doctor maybe they can help her. If she actually lets someone else in on this secret maybe I won't have to hold things together all by myself forever.

When she's done her call we all squeeze onto the couch and watch TV. I'm secretly hoping we'll get a chance to catch some *Degrassi*, but it's not on so we just watch a bunch of cartoons on the cartoon channel.

I look over at Mom. She just looks vaguely upset, which is pretty close to how she would actually look if she was in a normal Mom state and watching cartoons all day. I choose to take it as a good sign.

"What's she doing?" Henry asks as we finish up the dinner dishes later that night and head through the dining room to go upstairs. He's looking at Mom, who's back to staring at her hands.

"Nothing," I say.

"What do you mean?"

"Well, it used to be she had that face when she was thinking about Grandpa James being dead, but a couple days ago she told me she wasn't thinking about anything anymore."

"Oh," Henry says.

"Yeah," I reply.

We're back in my room and sitting on my bed and all of a sudden the sound of my cellphone ringing invades the silence. It's on my bedside table, and I dive for it and land hard on my side, which knocks the wind out of me.

"Hello?" I say, breathless.

"Oh, Julie, hi! How are you, dear?" It's Mrs. Greenwood.

"Oh, hi, Mrs. Greenwood!" I say, trying to sound as perky as she does.

"I'm just wondering if I can talk to Lorelei quickly. I made an appointment for the salon on Friday before the dance, and I wanted to confirm."

I pause, unsure what to say, my mind working quickly to catch up with the conversation.

"Actually, she's just in the washroom. Can I get her to call you back?" I ask.

Henry's watching me, and his eyes go wide, then narrow.

"Of course, dear, no problem. How are you? I saw you and your mother in the paper. What a misadventure. She's such a hero!"

My mom the superhero. I feel proud and sad at the same time.

"I'm fine. We're fine, thank you—just recovering, you know."

"Of course. Well, just get my daughter to call me when she comes back!"

"For sure, Mrs. Greenwood."

"Thank you, Julie. You're such a sweetheart!"

We say our goodbyes and I hang up. Then I hold a finger up to Henry as I dial Lorelei's cellphone number. It rings and rings and finally she picks up, sounding completely out of breath.

"Oh, hi, Julie," she says.

"Where are you?" I ask.

"Just over at Sammy's place getting the booze." She whispers the word *booze* again like we're back on the stage at school with Mrs. Singh right around the corner.

"Well, your mom thinks you're here and she just called about a salon appointment, so you have to call her back," I say.

"Oh, perfect. That's for the dance. I'm getting my hair done and nails and everything," she says.

"Why didn't you tell me I was supposed to cover for you? I got caught off guard," I say.

At this point I'm flat out avoiding Henry's glare.

"Well, you *did* cover for me, right?" she asks, nervous all of a sudden.

"Yeah."

"So no biggie then." I can feel the force of her smile through the phone, but it doesn't help make me less angry. There, I said it. I'm angry.

"It's just that I would have preferred some warning," I say.

"Oh, dahling, I just knew you could improvise.

230

No biggie," she says. I hear some shuffling in the background and then a cough, which I assume is stupid Sammy, his arms full of stupid booze as he tries to seduce Lorelei.

"Do you want to hang out tomorrow?" I ask. "My dad's coming home, but I'm sure he wouldn't mind if you came over to study." I really do need to hit the books; I can't keep slipping further and further behind. Maybe it will be a good incentive to study if I know I'm helping to save Lorelei from boarding school.

I shoot a glare over to Henry, who I can practically feel gawking at me. He makes a kissy face and rolls his eyes and I try not to laugh.

"I can't. I actually do have to study, but I obviously had to drop by Sammy's today or else I wouldn't have been able to get the stuff at all," Lorelei says. My heart plummets a bit and I sink into the bed. "I'll be by in a bit to drop off the booze. I'm leaving now, but I can't stay or anything," she continues.

"Okay, I guess I'll see you in a bit then," I say.

"For sure."

"Okay, bye."

"Bye."

"What was that all about?" Henry asks after I've put the phone back down onto my bedside table.

"She's out with Jamal's brother getting booze for the dance," I say.

He laughs. "Oh, right, that will go over well—a bunch of drunk high-schoolers surrounded by teachers."

"Exactly what I thought." I slide sideways on the bed until I'm next to him and the sides of our thighs are touching. It doesn't feel as good as touching Lorelei, but it doesn't feel bad either. His leg is kind of warm and the heat of it travels to my toes. "Anyway, she's coming by soon to drop it off here."

"Here? Why?"

"Well, her dad's threatening to send her away, so she can't get caught with it."

"Boarding school," Henry says.

"You know about that?" I ask.

"She mentioned it when we were going out. She seemed kind of embarrassed though, like she didn't want to talk about it."

"Yeah." I don't want to blab to Henry about Lorelei's slipping grades, so I don't say anything else. It's not my secret to tell.

We're quiet for a moment, then I ask, "Do you think Lorelei would hook up with Jamal's brother?"

"Do you want me to tell the truth?" he says.

It's an odd question, but it's the right question.

"Yes, truth," I say.

"Then yes."

There's a tightness in my chest, but at the same time I feel strangely relaxed. It's not some huge surprise, but the old feelings of jealousy come bubbling up like fizz popping in my brain.

"Did you love her?" I ask.

"Yeah, I think I did," Henry says.

"Why?"

"Um, I dunno . . . I guess because she was beautiful and confident and she made me feel special when she was looking at me. Come to think of it, it was all pretty shallow."

"We're best friends," I say, "so it's different with us." At least I think it's different. "I've just got to get up the nerve to actually, you know, ask her out for real."

"That's cool. I'm glad," Henry says, but he doesn't sound entirely glad. "Because you're both great and deserve great things. She's probably not hooking up with Sammy anyway, because he's way older and she's underage. They call girls like her jailbait."

"Really?" I say.

"Yup."

Even though I think he's lying it makes me feel better. Something in me is torn. I want to be able to let go of Lorelei, but at the same time I feel desperate to hold on tight.

My phone buzzes then with a text. It's from Lorelei. She's outside with the booze and she wants to pass it off to me. It all feels very clandestine, and I guess I should be excited to be helping, but I'm not.

I tell Henry to wait in my room and run down-stairs to meet her.

When I open the door she smiles wide and hands me a duffle bag that's weighed down with bottles. I don't tell her about Henry being upstairs, even though I feel like I should. But I don't want her to make a big deal out of it.

"I can't believe I'm doing this," I say instead.

"I knew I could count on you, dahling." Her face is flushed and her eyes are bright and sparkly, even in the dim streetlight. "I've got to run, but I'll see you Monday, okay?"

She leans over and gives me two kisses, one on each cheek, and the feeling of her lips lingers as I watch her walk away. But the feeling isn't all electric like it was when we kissed in her room that afternoon before the party. It's muted now, duller.

I lug the duffle bag up to my room, past my mom, who is still in the dining room, sitting in silence. If she was being my normal mom she might ask what I have in the bag. Then I would have to lie to her, so I'm kind of glad right this second that she's not being normal. I feel horrible thinking that, but it's true.

When I get back to my room, Henry is still sitting on my bed. He's picked up a book from my bedside table, school reading for English. He puts it down when he sees me.

"So, let's take a look," he says.

I lay the bag between us on the bed—it clinks and clanks when I move it—then I unzip the zipper. There are three bottles of Smirnoff in it, each about as tall as my forearm.

"Wow, that's a lot," I say. "I think."

"So, you have to keep it here till the dance?" Henry asks.

I shrug. "I should just pour it down the drain," I say, laughing.

He laughs too. "God, Lorelei would freak. You should do it."

"Seriously?" I run my fingers over the bottles. "I mean, I do think this is the worst idea ever. We could all get in so much trouble. Especially Lorelei. I don't want her to be shipped off to boarding school because of this."

"So you'd be saving her and yourself a big head-ache in the long run."

"Literally," I say, laughing again.

He grins at me and I zip up the bag and shove it under my bed.

"I'll think about it," I say. "In the meantime, I guess we should go to sleep."

"Okay," Henry replies.

And this time there's no cuddling or breathing in my ear. We build a pillow wall and sleep on either side.

13.

When I was thirteen I walked in on my mom and dad having sex. I was obviously mortified, but what followed was even worse. Mom and I had to "have the talk." It's not like I didn't know about sex, but Mom took it upon herself to teach me anyway. It was comprehensive. Mom provided anatomical pictures. I think she even had notes from her old sex-ed class. As embarrassing as it was, it was actually way better than high-school sex-ed.

It was so warm that at some point during the night I climbed on top of the bedding and shed Henry's sweatshirt, so I'm just in a tank top and shorts when I wake up. The pillow wall has fallen apart, and I'm not wearing enough clothing to be considered decent. Luckily Henry is still sleeping, so despite the heat I wriggle back into his sweatshirt. Then I lie down again and watch him sleep. It's probably pretty creepy, but he's in my bed so I figure I'm allowed. I guess I'm fine now with admitting that he's pretty cute—I try to imagine kissing him, but all I can picture is Lorelei's lips.

Then Henry's eyes open and I blush because he thinks I've been watching him, which I totally have.

"Why are you watching me sleep?" he says.

"You were talking," I say, which is a complete lie.

"Oh." He sounds sad. "Did I say anything interesting?"

"Naw, just gibberish. I'm famished," I say, rolling over and clutching my stomach dramatically.

"I can make eggs," he says.

"My dad is coming home this afternoon," I reply. It's definitely a jerky way to tell him he has to leave—just dropping a hint and hoping he gets it.

"Well, I should go home after breakfast," he says. "I wonder if my dad even noticed I wasn't there?" He laughs, but I don't. How could I laugh at that?

He reaches out and puts a hand on my shoulder. "Don't look so depressed."

"Eggs sounds good," I say, flashing him a huge smile.

Downstairs, Mom is still sitting at the dining-room table, where she's possibly been for the whole night. I want to scream.

Henry's eggs help calm me down though—they're amazing. In fact, everything he cooks is amazing. Now

I wish I knew more than how to bake a few cupcakes in my childhood Easy-Bake Oven that I still secretly use. We eat in silence and Mom gets up to feed JC, and for a little while everything feels strangely normal.

When we're done, Henry and I do the dishes. Then we stand around by the front door for a bit, kicking invisible pebbles and not wanting to say good-bye. After a long, uncomfortable silence Henry grabs my hands and pulls me into this huge, warm hug and whispers, "Thank you, Julie." But instead of letting him go I hug him back and squeeze him really hard.

Finally he extricates himself from my arms and we smile at each other.

"I'll see you at school," he says. His voice wobbles a little and cracks sadly. I don't want to send him home to what amounts to an empty house. I hold up a hand to stop him from leaving but instead I just wave good-bye. I watch him walk down the street. He doesn't turn back or anything.

When I get back to my room I think about what Henry and I talked about yesterday and pull the duffle bag out from under my bed. I unzip it and look at the three full bottles of vodka just sitting there. They look so innocent, completely unaware of all the trouble they'll cause later this week at the dance. I can't imagine it will all go as smoothly as Lorelei hopes. Then I think about that conversation Dad and I had in the car on the way home from the hospital. He didn't want Mom to run into Mr. Wellington's house. He said sometimes the right thing is debatable. So is that the case here? Is it right to disappoint Lorelei and pour the vodka down the drain? Or is it right to do nothing and let everyone at the dance get drunk and probably in trouble—to allow Lorelei to get sent off to boarding school? I try to think of what Mom would do.

She would run into the burning building.

She would be the superhero.

I take the bag into the bathroom and pour each of the bottles out into the sink. I feel a rush of guilt as I do, but I don't stop; I just keep pouring until they're all empty.

Lorelei is never going to forgive me for this.

The vodka stinks like crazy so I have to run the taps on hot for a couple of minutes and pump a bunch of hand soap into the sink. Then I fill each bottle with water and twist the caps back on as tight as they'll go. It probably won't fool Lorelei, but maybe if she doesn't notice the bottles are already open she'll think the punch is spiked and she won't hate me forever and ever. Either way it's worth the risk if it means her not getting sent away.

When I'm finished and I've repacked the bottles into the duffle bag, I go back to my room and put the bag back under my bed. At this point I'm not really sure what to do with myself. With all the stress piled up on me there's no way I can study, so I just lie on my bed wrapped in Henry's sweatshirt until I finally hear the sound of Dad coming home from La La Land.

I try to make the reunion as joyous as possible. I bound down the stairs and hug Dad, then pick up JC and help Mom up from her seat at the table. It's supposed to be rousing and exciting, but it all feels like this time in grade four when we put on a puppet play and I had to play five different characters because everybody got sick with the chicken pox and had to stay home. Mom and JC are my puppets, and I jiggle them around in Dad's face while he smiles and pretends the whole thing isn't one big act.

Dad brought us some stuff from La La Land, including a snow globe, which is actually a sand globe. He also brought a bunch of beach towels and American candy he picked up at the airport's duty-free shop. It's all so colourful and bright—meant to make us forget that Mom is dead and nothing is as it should be.

"How was your flight?" Mom asks, doing her best impression of Mom.

"It was long, and I missed you all so much." Dad's rendition of himself is flawless, except that I think the dash of grey in his hair is expanding exponentially.

"Did you do lots of boring computer stuff?" I ask.

He laughs. "You know it, honey." He gives me another hug, but this time he holds me longer than before. I hug him back and nuzzle in deep under his chin where he's grown a mini-beard for the first time in forever.

"I like your beard," I say. "Very lumberjack chic."

He laughs again. "How is everything here?"

I know I could tell him about school and Lorelei and Henry, but that's not what he wants to hear. He wants to know if Mom went to therapy, or if she jumped into any more burning buildings. My problems with my love life and Henry's problems at home are a million miles away right now. All Dad wants to know is if everything is going to be all right.

"Things are good, Dad," I say in my most reassuring voice. I feel bad about lying to him, but he looks so tired, and I really don't want to put any more stress on him than he already has. Plus, Mom made a new appointment for the shrink, so I have it under control. "I cut Mom's hair and we even watched cartoons." I'm not actually sure Mom watching cartoons is a sign that things are good, so I immediately regret saying it. Dad ignores it, though, and looks at Mom, who is sitting down again. He smiles really wide in this I'm-smiling-at-an-infant sort of way and says, "Olive, your hair looks wonderful!"

And Mom reiterates, "Julie has a way with hair."

Then Dad turns to me and pulls me to the side conspiratorially. "Did she go to her session?"

"Yeah, and I think it helped," I say. My chest feels tight, like all the secrets and lies are filling my lungs and at some point will just burst out of my mouth and into the world. We both look at Mom, who is staring down at JC like he's a strange creature she's never seen before. "Sort of."

"I'm so sorry I had to do this to you, Julie," Dad says.

"I told you I was okay." I put my hand on his shoulder to reassure him. I wish he didn't have to leave, and I wish I didn't have to be in charge of Mom all the time, but I don't want him to stress out either.

"Maybe, but that's not the point. You shouldn't just have to be okay. *We* shouldn't *just* be okay."

We hug again, longer this time, and lean into each other. He's right. We shouldn't *just* be okay. I wish we could be back to normal, and maybe if Mom *actually* goes to the shrink we can be.

For dinner we have Chinese, and Mom pushes her chow mein around on her plate but doesn't eat any. I eat way too much lemon chicken, and Dad tells us about the beach that he only got to set foot on once, and the fact that he may have seen Cate Blanchett at Starbucks, but he's not one hundred percent sure.

Lorelei loves this kind of stuff: I imagine her all starry-eyed and swooning over the celebrity sighting when I tell her.

After I do the dishes and change JC, I head to my room and try to do some homework before bed. But of course I can't focus on my work.

A few minutes after I turn out the lights and crawl into bed, I hear a couple of creaks and then the crack of my door. Dad comes in and sits down on the bed. I stick my hand out from under my covers so he can grab it.

"I wasn't done with our conversation," Dad says. His shoulders are curved forward and in.

"Now that your mom is going to the doctor I hope she'll be a little less . . . " He doesn't want to say *crazy*, because that's a loaded word, but *crazy* is the word for it. There's a long, dark pause, like the whole room is holding its breath, and then Dad just sighs instead of finishing his sentence. I feel terrible not telling him about the missed appointment, about the graveyard visit, about the crappy eulogy I tried to make up for her. Mom *was* a wonderful person. Mom *made* amazing macaroni.

"Yeah," I say brightly instead. As if everything is totally going to be fine. "You sound tired."

He laughs quietly. "I am. It was a long flight."

"Do you have to go to work tomorrow?" I ask.

"You know it, kiddo."

I shake my head and make a frowny face and he leans over to give me a hug. He smells like freshly showered Dad, and his beard is gone.

"I really did like the beard," I say.

"Sorry, honey, it was driving me nuts."

"Goodnight, Dad."

"Night."

Then creak, creak, creak and he's gone.

On Monday the feeling at school is tense and hormonal because of the upcoming dance. Lorelei is in full planner mode and she's gotten really bossy. She's always up to something dance-wise: yelling at Josie about the streamers or making secret hand gestures to Sheila about getting the booze into the punch bowl at exactly the right moment. I feel guilty every time I see her and Sheila gesturing to each other, but I don't regret what I've done.

The teachers are completely tense too. Mr. Gomez is looking extra eagle-nosed, and Mrs. Singh is following me around constantly and checking in with me to make sure everything is all right. Henry is outside as usual during lunch, and he stops by our table a couple of times to say hi. The second time he comes by Lorelei has gone in to use the bathroom, and I'm grateful for the chance to talk to him alone.

"So . . . is everything okay?" I ask. "I tried texting you yesterday, but I never heard back."

He grins wide, balancing the ball on his hip again. "My dad was actually mad. It was kind of great."

I want to jump up and hug him, but I stay seated and offer a big smile instead. "That's amazing."

"Yeah. He took away my phone and he grounded me, but whatever—at least he's talking to me."

My heart drops into my stomach. Grounded? "What about the dance?" I ask.

Henry frowns and kicks the ground a little. "I'm going to try and make it."

"But you have to!" I'm almost shouting now. I've got to calm down; I am way too worked up about this.

Henry laughs. "I'm glad you're so concerned for me."

I roll my eyes and take a deep breath. "You promised me a dance," I said.

He squares his shoulders and looks me in the eye. "I know. And I will make good on that promise."

My cheeks burst into flames and I look down at my lunch, trying to avoid his gaze. Luckily, at that moment Lorelei comes back from the bathroom and plunks herself down across from me.

"Hi, Henry," she says breezily.

"I was just heading back to practice," Henry replies.

"Mmm hmm," she says.

"Bye," I whisper.

When he runs off Lorelei locks her eyes on me and folds her hands in front of her on the table. "What was all that about?" she asks.

I shake my head, trying to dislodge the feeling of disappointment over the fact that Henry might not come to the dance.

"Nothing," I say, and shove a huge bite of soggy egg salad into my mouth.

"Sure," Lorelei replies, laughing.

After school, as soon as I walk in the front door at home, something feels horribly familiar.

The blood-curdling baby screams from upstairs in JC's room.

The stillness that wouldn't be so still if Mom was really around.

It reminds me of the day I walked into the kitchen and found Mom staring blindly out the window. *I can't feel my heartbeat.* This time I'm not so tentative though. I may not be a superhero, but I'm not the same scared girl I was a couple of weeks ago. I run through the house. I start in the kitchen and quickly make my way through every room before I head upstairs to take care of JC. He smiles when he sees me, but he also stinks.

When I'm done changing him I go to Mom's room and then check my own, but she's not there. There's probably only one last place she could be other than out, but I really, really don't want to go there.

I creak downstairs and place JC in his basket. I give him his donkey, which hee-haws in a way that should be cute but is eerie in the silent house. Then I brace myself. I head through the kitchen and into the pantry, around the corner and down into the basement. I only go to the basement on rare occasions, when Mom or Dad basically forces me down there to get something from the extra freezer or the crawl space. As I said before, it's not exactly that I am afraid of it; it's more that I'm worried about the potential for coming into contact with certain airborne damp-condition bacteria. So as I descend down the creaky old gnarly wooden-slat stairs, I hold my breath.

It's dark in the basement despite dim light filtering in through a couple of ragged windows. The single light bulb down there is supposed to illuminate the whole room, but it does a pretty pathetic job. The whole space is gross and dank and smells like wet stone.

And here I am looking at the one thing I had hoped never to see again.

Straight from the Casket Cathedral, by way of Violet, no doubt, here on the ground in the basement is my mom's final resting place. The metal coffin looks dull grey in the low light, and it's just sitting on the floor like it's been there all along.

Everything in me feels tight and heavy, like I'm wearing too many clothes. I forget to hold my breath and breathe deep, my lungs filling with damp air. And when I exhale I sob a little. I hate seeing this thing here in my house. I can't understand how this is happening, and I wish more than anything that when I open the casket I won't find my mom inside.

But of course I do. The hinge doesn't creak; it just makes a light whooshing sound, and instead of the smell of decay and rotten body parts, it's the smell of new car that hits me as I open it. And, of course, my pale mom is tucked in there, eyes closed and hands on her chest like some stupid old-time horror-movie vampire.

"Mom, you can't have a coffin in the basement," I say, my voice tense and my body hunched tightly over her. "Dad's going to find out, and it won't be me who told him. It'll be him seeing it on the credit card bill or him coming down here for something and stubbing his toe. I'm trying to keep your secret, but you have to work with me."

Mom opens her eyes and looks up at me. For a second I think she's going to reach out and touch my face, but she just keeps her hands where they are and says, "This is where I belong." She speaks so quietly I can barely hear her without leaning farther into the stupid coffin.

I shake my head and try not to yell or kick or pull her out onto the grungy floor. "No, Mom, you belong upstairs with us. Remember—you're a hero! You're going to go to therapy and you're a wonderful person with a lot left to do."

"I *was* a wonderful person," she says, even more quietly.

"Not past tense, Mom. If you *were* a wonderful person, how are you still talking to me now? That means you're *currently* a wonderful person. *In the process* of being a wonderful person. Present tense." My throat is tight, all closed up with stress and sadness. I'm trying not to cry.

This time she does reach out, and she grabs my hand and pulls it down to her chest. "See? No heartbeat." Her words are like thin slices of air, barely making it to my ears.

I feel a faint pulse under her rib cage, thump-thumping like any normal heart should.

"Dad's going to be home soon, and we can make him dinner together. What should we make?" I ask. I'm trying to change the subject, make this normal.

"Julie, I'm falling apart. This is where I belong. I need you to bury me beside Grandpa James. I miss him and he misses me." She says this a little louder, more insistently, her eyes roaming across my face.

"Yeah, well, you don't believe in an afterlife, so what do you think's going to happen when I bury you, Mom? You think you'll just fly up to heaven and there'll be clouds and angels and you can touch the face of God?" I'm yelling now, and I'm sure it's going to upset JC, but I can't help it. All the sadness is draining out of me and turning into anger as I speak. "Heaven is just an idea, Mom, it's a metaphor . . . but you need to be thinking about me now. Me and JC and Dad. That's what matters."

Mom is still clutching my hand to her heart, and it's thump-thumping faster now. I want to feel it go faster and faster, so I just keep yelling at her. "You have to get up and be a hero because I'm not a hero at all. There are like a billion people out there who have crappy moments in their lives, but they don't go lying around in coffins being all melodramatic about it. You can save so many people. When JC gets older, you will be a firefighter again and you can run in to all sorts of burning buildings like you did for Mr. Wellington. So you should just get up and do that and we'll make macaroni together because I want to learn how to cook, okay?"

Her heart is really pumping now, but she's not moving; she's just staring at me like she's forgotten my name. So I grab her arms and haul her out of the stupid metal coffin and onto her feet.

"And who gets a metal coffin anyway, Mom? Doesn't that, like, go against some sort of law of nature or something? Isn't it bad for the environment?" But I don't wait for her to respond. Instead I just push her lightly up the stairs and into the kitchen, where I sit her on a stool and demand that she teach me how to make macaroni and cheese.

On Friday the school is even more abuzz with excitement about the dance. I have to admit to my own excitement too, but it's tainted by Mom's downward spiral. I thought I was getting somewhere by having her agree to therapy, and then she goes and buys a stupid coffin. I'm going to have to do something about it before Dad finds it and flips his lid. Maybe I can contact Violet at the Casket Despot and get her to take it back. Is there even a return policy for coffins?

Lorelei is still going all out with the dance planning; she dug up some walkie-talkies from the computer lab and has handed them out to all her volunteers (a.k.a. lackeys). She's constantly barking orders into channel nine, which makes everyone in the class roll their eyes while Mr. Gomez ignores it completely as he struggles to teach through the haze of hormones. Today is

UN again, and everyone is extra shouty. They're fighting like wild beasts over a trade route in the Arctic that's owned by about five different countries, none of which is Congo.

In the midst of all the chaos Lorelei leans over to my desk, her hair brushing against my fingers, and whispers, "So we'll come by your place to pick you up at three thirty, then we'll get dressed at your house after the salon?"

I'm surprised; I thought the salon was a mother/daughter experience for her and Mrs. Greenwood. I raise my eyebrows at her and she smiles, the corners of her lips curling up like a piece of paper that's been lit on fire.

"I told Mother there was absolutely no way I was going to the salon without you, so she booked a spot for you and your mom too."

I nod and look down at my fingernails. They're chewed to the skin after a long week of worry. "I don't think my mom can make it," I say. But Lorelei doesn't hear me; she just leans away from me and shouts something about paper cups into her walkie-talkie. It's fine. They can pick me up and I'll just make up some excuse for Mom. There's no way she's in any shape to go out with Lorelei and her mom. What would she do—get her pale face done up with creams and peels? Tell Mrs. Greenwood about her amazing new coffin? The thought makes me want to puke.

I've never been to the salon for a makeover before. Mom and I are more moviegoers or park walkers, not salon ladies who sit and gossip under those big round heat helmets like catty deep-sea divers. I try to picture myself having fun while someone saws away at my fingers with an emery board, but the thought gives me the shivers. I thought I would just borrow a dress and wing it, but Lorelei is smiling so hard I can't help but be happy that she wants me there by her side while she's getting plastered in seaweed masks and plucked like a chicken. I feel like we've been drifting apart since the whole thing with Mr. Gomez and with all the secrets I've been keeping from her: about Henry, about my mom. So maybe this dance will be the boost we need to reconnect, and I can focus on my feelings, really figure out if I'm still in love with her.

We spend all of lunch setting up the gym, but I manage to sneak out to the schoolyard to find Henry. I want to ask him if anything has changed, to confirm whether or not he will be at the dance. I spot him out in the middle of the field, as usual, running and kicking the ball with his team. He doesn't notice me and I don't want to interrupt him, so I just head back to the gym where Lorelei is yelling like crazy at the troops about streamer placement.

. . .

When I get home, JC is crying again because Mom is back in the basement on vampire duty—eyes closed, silent and ghostly. This is how it's been all week, she's spending more and more time in there, and it's getting harder to get her out when I get home from school. If things keep up like this I'm going to have to start carrying her up the basement stairs.

"Mom, I'm going to the salon at three thirty," I say, "so you have to get up and deal with JC, okay?"

She resists when I try to get her up, so I pull and pull. JC squirms when I try to change him, so I push and push. It's overwhelming, and there is a pit of stress growing in my stomach.

The doorbell rings when I am up in my room and I race downstairs to get it. I pass the dining room on the way, where Mom is at the table, of course, looking at her hands. At least she hasn't crawled back into her stupid coffin.

It's Lorelei and Mrs. Greenwood.

"Julie, dahling!" Mrs. Greenwood says, stepping into the house and pulling me into a hug. She still smells like lemon and hairspray. It's a nice, normal Mom smell and it tugs at my heart.

"Hi, Mrs. Greenwood," I say.

"Where's Olive and that sweet little baby of hers?" she asks. She just sort of pushes past me and charges into the house before I can respond.

"Oh, she can't make it," I call after her. But she's already turned the corner into the dining room. Lorelei follows her in, rolling her eyes in a dramatic fashion.

"Sorry about Mother," she says. "She just gets excited."

"Olive! Lovely to see you! Are you ready to go?"

I race to catch up with them, trying hard to think of some kind of excuse for Mom. Like maybe she has some sort of sleeping sickness, or she twisted her ankle, or she has a very important appointment she has to keep—a doctor? A lawyer? What would be the thing that would lead to the fewest questions?

But before I can say any of it, I round the corner into the dining room and see Mom standing behind her chair, all straight-backed and pale, looking like she's just risen for the national anthem. And here is Mrs. Greenwood, rushing over to her and grabbing her by her stick-thin arm, pulling her gently toward the front door.

"This is going to be so much fun, isn't it, Olive?" Mrs. Greenwood chatters. "Have you ever been to the spa? Do you want me to carry the baby, or should we have the girls take care of him? How have you been? You look so different than the last time I saw you! Have you lost some weight?"

Mom doesn't say a word in response, but that doesn't seem to matter to Mrs. Greenwood. She just keeps chirping away like a little bird and escorting my mom out of the house toward her car.

"My mom's just really tired," I say to Lorelei desperately. "I'm not sure she can really come."

But Lorelei just laughs and tells me, "Don't worry, dahling."

So I grab JC's basket and we're off downtown to this fancy salon in Yorkville.

When we get there I realize it's probably not the best place to bring a baby—it reeks like toxic chemicals and the hair dryers are really loud. But it's okay because Lorelei and Mrs. Greenwood are there, and their smiles have the same effect as the walls in Lorelei's room: they make me happy no matter how much the manicurist digs into my cuticles or the hairdresser pulls at my scalp with the straightener.

"Isn't this fun? A real girls' afternoon out," Mrs. Greenwood says, hair rising on a wave of hairspray and heat. "Except for James Christopher, of course, but he can be an honorary girl for the day, can't he?" Mrs. Greenwood refuses to call my brother JC, and I think it's probably because of the religious connotations. It doesn't make sense to me though—I know religious people name their kids after saints and prophets and stuff all the time, so why not the J-Man himself?

"You'll give him a complex by calling him a girl, Mother," Lorelei says. She's getting her nails painted silver, which almost matches the current colour of her eyes. I doubt that's even true. It's not like babies understand gender identity. Plus, I'm sure he'd think it was fine to be considered one of the girls today, if he even cared at all.

"Oh, I'm so excited for you girls," Mrs. Greenwood says, ignoring her. "High school was such a lovely time for me. Wasn't it a lovely time for you, Olive?"

Mom is staring at her hands again, which is actually kind of fitting this time because her nails are getting shellacked with glittery polish. She doesn't respond to Mrs. Greenwood.

"Mom?" I say, raising my voice above the drone of the hair dryers. I feel like I'm back at the puppet show—I wish I could make my mom talk and dance for the audience.

Mom looks up and over at Mrs. Greenwood. "Oh, yes," she says.

I'm pretty horrified by her lack of a defined answer, but Mrs. Greenwood just beams, clearly thrilled at Mom's conversational prowess. "And that article in the paper? I read it—how thrilling!" she says.

"Oh, yes," my mom says once more.

"Yeah, Mom is thrilled. She's just tired from all the heroics," I say. Then I laugh to try to cover up Mom's complete lack of enthusiasm.

But thankfully Mrs. Greenwood is oblivious. Still

beaming, she bends over to remove her shoes for the pedi part of the mani-pedi.

It takes an awfully long time to get done up just right. It's past six by the time we get out of the salon. Mom looks a bit healthier than usual given the amount of makeup they slathered on her, and Lorelei is positively glowing as we drive home. When we get to my house Lorelei and her mother do this air-kissing thing on both sides of the face that Lorelei claims is very European, and Mrs. Greenwood tells us to have the best time ever but to stay away from the boys because they'll expect things of us when we're all dolled up. Lorelei rolls her eyes.

I guide Mom out of the car carefully, and Mrs. Greenwood says, "Let's get together soon, Olive!" And my mom says, "Oh, yes," like those are the only two words left in the English language that she knows. Once we've waved goodbye to Mrs. Greenwood and set Mom up in the dining room with JC, we go upstairs to my room to change. I kind of worry that once we're alone Lorelei will make a big deal out of my mom acting totally weird the whole time we were at the salon. But thankfully, just like Mrs. Greenwood, she seems totally oblivious and carries on like nothing is amiss.

Lorelei got a new dress especially for this occasion. It's a silver tube dress with a hole for the belly button and a couple of horizontal slits along the back.

I'm wearing her red dress—Henry's apparent favourite. It slips up my legs and lingers near my butt, but it's not nearly as short as Lorelei's. I definitely know now why she wanted to come here to get changed. There's not a chance her parents would let her wear that dress anywhere except maybe her room, but even then with the blinds closed, and even then probably not at all. Lorelei grabs me and spins me around and her dress feels smooth and slippery, like some sort of silver space-eel. I feel almost frumpy standing next to her, even though my hair is up in a nice way and my nails are like cartoon cherries that look good enough to eat.

"We look so hot," she says. She's practically supersonic with excitement. I'm happy because she's happy, but there are circumstances keeping me from being totally thrilled. The knot of stress is still sitting in my stomach like a stone, making me a bit queasy. On top of everything with Mom, I'm worried about what Lorelei will do if she doesn't fall for my water-in-the-vodka-bottles trick.

"Everyone's gonna drool over us," she says.

"Like who?" I ask.

She shrugs and sighs and hair flips in this glorious trifecta of drama. "It doesn't matter *who*—it's that everyone will be drooling. The whole room will be looking and jealous and lusty."

I hear the sound of a phone buzzing and my heart leaps a little in my chest because I think it might be Henry finally texting me back. But it's Lorelei's phone, not mine. She sits down on my bed while she types out her response.

"Who is it?" I ask, flopping down beside her and looking at the screen.

She yanks the phone up to her chest, but not fast enough that I don't see her message.

Lorelei: Can't wait to see you tonight. <3

My mouth falls open and my throat closes up.

Is Lorelei in a relationship I don't know about? I didn't get a chance to see who she was texting. I want to ask, but I feel like my voice has been sucked right out of my throat. All my old feelings of jealousy rise up, bubbling away in my stomach. Lorelei's silver-green eyes are locked on me; she's obviously waiting for me to say something. To know how much I saw.

"Who . . . was that?" I finally manage.

She clicks off her phone and puts it on the bed, face down. Then she grabs onto my hands.

"Listen, dahling," she whispers. "Don't worry about it, okay?"

"Why won't you tell me?" I try to flip through memories in my mind. Is there someone she's been hanging out with more than usual? I try to imagine her walking down the hall, holding hands with—who?

She looks down at my comforter. Is that guilt I see on her face? Embarrassment? I don't know. The expression is so unfamiliar, so un-Lorelei.

"I can't talk about it, okay? I just need you to drop it, Julie." She sounds dead serious, more serious than I have ever heard her before.

"Okay, but it's not such a big deal, you know. You can tell me if you have a boyfriend or something." I'm not even sure if what I'm saying is true. *Is* it a big deal to me? I still feel a steady pulse of jealousy curling around in my stomach, but it doesn't have the same intensity as it used to.

"I said drop it," Lorelei says, her voice getting high-pitched and angry.

"Okay." I hold up my hands and then drop them onto my legs. "Okay."

I stand up and try to shake all my feelings off. I yank my skirt down and it pops back up again.

Then I hear my dad come home. Suddenly the image of Mom in the coffin jumps into my mind, and I hope that she didn't escape down into it when I left her alone with JC. But soon I hear the quiet rumble of conversation, so I know it's okay.

I look over at Lorelei and she smiles too brightly at me. "We should go," she says.

"We're going to have to wear sweaters when we leave," I tell her. "I don't want my dad complaining about the length of our dresses or anything."

Lorelei giggles like everything is back to normal, and kisses the air in front of my mouth because air-kisses won't mess up her lipstick. But everything isn't normal at all, and that stone in my stomach is turning into a boulder.

"Of course, dahling. I thought of everything." She pulls two silk kimonos out of her bag. They fall practically to the floor with these long flowing sleeves, and when I put mine on I imagine I'm a caterpillar in a cocoon.

"We can tell him kimonos are in this season," she says. Then she grabs her phone and slips it into her purse. She doesn't even look at it again. She's trying to pretend that nothing happened, I guess. That she's not keeping secrets from her best friend. Because that's what we are, right—best friends?

I pull the duffle bag out from under my bed, but it clinks so loudly I pause.

"We have to put something in here," I say. I grab a couple of sweaters and shove them in the bag to stop the bottles from clanking against each other.

"Good idea," Lorelei says excitedly.

I consider just telling her right then and there about what I did, how I poured the vodka down the drain. But I decide to take my chances with faking her out instead. I don't want to ruin the dance completely. It's still supposed to be fun.

In a cloud of glitter and perfume, we run down the stairs.

Dad insists on taking pictures of us, and I pass the duffle bag to Lorelei behind my back as we pose. Dad smiles wide, even though his eyes look like he's already fallen asleep.

Then he hugs me.

"Time moves so quickly," he says. "Don't grow up too fast, okay?"

I roll my eyes like a good teenager, but hug him tight.

14.

My mom got pregnant with JC when I was fourteen. It was a surprise to everyone, but we were all excited. Mom took maternity leave, and she was home all the time, like when I was little. She started doing all these Mom-things again, like baking cookies and making these huge, elaborate dinners instead of just the bare minimum. It was the first time I remember thinking of her as more than just my mom. She looked so out of place in the kitchen with an apron on. I started asking about her life before she had me, and she told me stories about wild parties, high-school boyfriends, meeting my dad at a bar and falling in love. She was so much more than the person who held me when I was sick.

Mom drives us to the dance and we arrive at 7:00 p.m. on the dot. She drops us off in the parking lot and we wave goodbye as we join the herd of partygoers heading into the school. I turn around to watch her drive away. I'm still so worried about her driving on her own. Will she just go off to the grave-yard now? Or will she go home and at least try to act normal? The boulder in my stomach rolls around a bit and I try to tamp down the nausea it causes.

As Lorelei grabs my hand and pulls me along to the door, I resolve to put my mom out of my mind for the night.

Just one night to myself.

Just one night to have fun and not think about cof-fins and eulogies and graveyards.

Tomorrow I'll make plans to return the coffin. I'll make sure she goes to therapy.

But tonight is just for me.

The principal greets us and we keep our kimonos on until we make our big entrance. Lorelei wants to make sure no one freaks out before we get the chance to show some skin. She grabs my hand and we filter into the gym. It looks incredibly church-like; rainbow spotlights shining down like stained glass onto the floor and streamers running like rafters up to the ceil-ing give it a vaulted effect. I scan the growing crowd for Henry, but he's not here yet . . . if he's even coming.

We make an immediate beeline for the drinks table, and Lorelei shoves the duffle bag underneath. Luckily she planned ahead and chose a long tablecloth that goes all the way to the floor. Lorelei wants to wait for the gym to get crowded before we pour the booze. She thinks it will be easier to hide it that way, and we definitely have to wait for Sheila to come and stand guard.

It's all planned out perfectly.

If she only knew.

A couple of teachers are here already, lingering awkwardly around the periphery; Mrs. Singh is wearing a gorgeous blue dress and Mr. Gomez is in a suit and golden tie that matches the ring around his eyes. When we make our way to the dance floor, Mrs. Singh spots me, of course, and waves a little. I wave back to be polite, but I hope she won't follow me around the whole night like she's been doing since the fire.

The gym is still relatively empty. Lorelei and I wait until the place has filled up a bit more before we shed our kimonos dramatically in the middle of the dance floor, like butterflies shucking our cocoons to reveal our delicate transformation. She gets some looks, and a bit of a murmur arises, but it dies quickly as a slow song comes on and everyone pairs off for the first official slow dance of the night.

Lorelei grabs onto me and twirls me around, then rocks me back and forth. I try to relax and push all the swirling thoughts out of my mind while we dance.

We're here to have fun, simple as that.

I force a grin at people as we sway: Nima and Gwen with their dates, Ed Simpson too, who is actually here with a guy who appears to be his boyfriend. Ed smiles back, but Nima and Gwen don't notice me. We pass Josie and Carla twirling across the floor together and I nod. Carla nods back and gives me a knowing wink, but Josie is too busy resting her head on Carla's shoulder to pay any attention to me.

"God," Lorelei says as we are swaying, "where is Sheila? She promised she would be here on time to guard the punch. This won't work without her."

I shrug and scan the crowd, but I'm not looking for Sheila. I'm looking for Henry. He did promise me that dance.

Then a fast song comes on and we all move together in a big jumble. That's how it is at dances during fast songs: everyone dances with everyone else. All the grades are squished together in the crowd, even though on a normal day the grade twelves would never brush shoulders with us lowly niners.

Lorelei is watching the crowd intensely now, making rounds of the dance floor and the tables close to the stage, looking for Sheila. She's pretty late, and Lorelei is starting to get really annoyed. Another slow song comes on and she comes back to dance with me, but I'm preoccupied too. I should be enjoying the feeling of dancing with Lorelei, but I'm too busy wondering about Henry.

Was he not able to get out of being grounded?

Both of our eyes are glued on the door, and we

bump into Jamal and his girlfriend, Gracie. We all laugh awkwardly.

"Sorry," I say.

Jamal and Gracie just shrug. "No worries," Jamal says.

"Have you heard from Henry?" I blurt at Jamal before I can stop myself. "I mean, do you know if he's coming?"

Jamal and Henry are on the soccer team together, and I'm pretty sure they're friends.

"Nope, I don't know. I mean, I know he's grounded, but he didn't say whether he would be out tonight," Jamal says.

I can't stop myself from frowning.

"Sorry," Jamal says.

"No . . . it's okay, thanks."

Lorelei has wandered off again, looking for Sheila, no doubt. So I kind of jiggle around on the dance floor by myself for a bit until she comes back. But I don't really feel like dancing with her anymore. I *feel* like dancing with Henry. Where is he?

Lorelei sweeps me into a tight hug for the next slow song and we both look over each other's shoulder toward the door. By the time the song is almost done, I'm considering stepping off the dance floor to try calling Henry, even though I know he got his phone taken away.

But then he appears in the doorway, dressed in a suit jacket and jeans.

A smile spreads through my whole body, and for a brief second the weight of the boulder in my stomach lifts.

"I'll be right back," I tell Lorelei, and she waves me off distractedly, eyes still wandering the gym.

I weave through the crowd and hurl myself at Henry like he's a net and I'm a soccer ball. I end up almost knocking him over, but he doesn't seem to mind. He hugs me so tight I feel like parts of me might burst.

"Hi," he says.

"You're late," I reply.

"It looks great in here. You guys did a good job."

"I thought you weren't going to make it."

He smiles. "Me too, actually. God, my dad was so mad at me. I begged him. I even promised he could have me for the next two weeks if he let me out tonight. He told me to have fun." He laughs. "I honestly never thought I could be so happy to be grounded."

"It's perfect," I say.

He smiles at me and my stomach flips. Then he looks around the room and I see him zero in on some of his soccer friends. "I'm going to go say hi, but I still want my dance," he says.

"Okay."

I scan the room for Lorelei and spot her over in a darkened corner talking to Mr. Gomez. The heaviness in my stomach returns instantaneously. I picture them together on his desk, so close. Closer than they're standing now, but just barely. Why does he always look like he's tripping and falling into her?

I head back out onto the dance floor and squirm around a bit with all the other kids who are pressed up against each other in a big smear of sweat and hands and hips. I try to put all the thoughts of Lorelei and Mr. Gomez out of my mind. Lorelei told me there was nothing going on, so I should believe her. After a little while Lorelei comes to find me.

"What were you talking to Mr. Gomez about?" I ask when the song turns slow and things get a bit quieter.

"I just wanted to see if he was having fun. What were you talking to Henry about?" Her eyes look sharp and silver under the rainbow lights.

"I was just saying hi," I reply.

"Cool," she says.

Then we put our heads on each other's shoulder and rock back and forth in the sea of slow-dancing couples. I smell her shampoo and feel the heat of her, but for the first time in forever I don't really want to kiss her. My mind keeps wandering all over the place: thinking about her and Mr. Gomez; my mom at home, pale and past tense; how happy I am that Henry came to the dance.

The night gets thicker and everyone get sweatier. The air smells like bodies and various perfumes mixed together in a stinky froth. Near the end of a mosh-pitty song Lorelei finally sees Sheila over by the drinks table and runs off to meet up with her. And my stress levels rise, because now is the moment she might find out what I did. I doubt she'll confront me in the middle of the dance, but if she doesn't fall for my little trick, I have no idea how it will affect our friendship.

With my body tense, my stomach heavy and my heart beating hard, the only person I want to see is Henry. I search the crowd and find him at a table with his soccer friends. I smile at them and offer Henry my hand for the slow song that comes next.

"You look nice," he says once we're on the dance floor, his arms wrapped tight around my waist.

"Lorelei says the red dress is your favourite."

"It's not," he replies. His breath is really warm in my ear, and it tickles. His arms feel different than Lorelei's—more sturdy, less soft.

"Really?" I say.

"Nope, the sweatshirt is my favourite."

"I should give it back. Sorry for having it for so long." The song picks up pace in the second half, but we stay slow dancing, swaying softly while the other kids around us move faster. Maybe the gravity of the both of us together is having some kind of temporal effect.

"No, it's my favourite on *you*," he says.

"Oh." I don't know what to say. I feel like my entire stomach has migrated to my knees, and it almost makes me want to kiss him. Either that or go pee.

"Sorry," he says.

"No . . . no, it's fine."

"I don't want to make it weird."

I think about the two of us in the graveyard, carrying my dead mom to the car. "It's way past weird at this point," I say. I have to work hard to push the image of Mom out of my head. I've been doing so well not thinking about her tonight. But Henry's blue, blue eyes help.

"Can I tell you something?" I ask.

"Always," he replies.

"I promised myself I would try not to think about it tonight, but I can't stop . . . "

He looks concerned, this cute little crease appearing between his eyebrows.

"My mom bought a coffin."

His face falls and he shakes his head slowly. "Shit."

"I know. I don't know what to do. I want to try to return it but—"

My sentence is cut short by a hand on my shoulder. Henry looks past me and his frown deepens. I turn around and Henry drops his arms, all the sturdy warmth of them suddenly lost.

Lorelei is behind me, practically on fire, her face is so bright red.

"What the fuck did you do, Julie?" The way she says my name makes it sound like it's the swear word. I take a step back, because her face is right in mine and her eyes are shooting scorching lasers at me.

"I had to be the hero," I whisper, my voice barely audible above the pounding music. I realize how stupid that sounds the second it comes out of my mouth, but it's the truth. The boulder is doing huge flips in my stomach, like it's rolling really fast down a steep hill.

"You are such a child. How could you do this to me?" Lorelei's voice is rising, and I feel like I'm shrinking under the weight of it. I didn't think she would do this here. I didn't think she would be this mad.

"This was supposed to be a perfect night and you had to go fuck everything up." She's practically screaming now. People have started to form a small circle around us, giving us some space.

"Lorelei, relax," Henry says. I turn to him. He's watching Lorelei calmly, his face completely neutral, like he deals with this kind of thing all the time.

Lorelei ignores him, her eyes still burning into me. "Why can't you just grow up and realize you're not the only person in the world? Other people have lives, have plans, and you can't just go ruining them because you're a complete coward," she says.

I feel a swell of anger rise in my chest. I was just trying to help. It was a terrible idea to spike the punch, and she could have gotten into so much trouble. "I was doing you a favour, saving you! What about your shitty grades? What about boarding school? I had to do something. I couldn't just sit back and watch you ruin the dance."

Her face looks distorted in the low light.

And that's when I realize I basically just told her secret to the whole school.

How could I have done that?

I was supposed to be the vault.

Lorelei throws her head back and laughs, her white teeth flashing rainbow under the lights. "Me, ruin the dance? *You* ruined the dance, Julie. You ruined everything."

I look around at the circle of faces on the dance floor. Some I recognize, some I don't. Nima and Ed, Sheila and Josie. A couple people have their phones out and are recording us. Great—our best-friend blow-up will be immortalized on the Internet now.

"Let's just go somewhere and talk about this, okay? Let me explain," I say. I feel bad for letting her secret slip. I just want to do something to save us both from making fools of ourselves. More than we already have.

But Lorelei isn't listening. She turns around and storms off the dance floor. I follow her quickly, pushing my way through the crowd. The music is still playing and I feel it in my chest, thumping along with my heartbeat.

Boom boom, boom boom.

Henry follows me and grabs onto my hand, and I drag him along with me. My stomach boulder is so heavy it's weighing me down, making me move slower and slower. Nothing feels like it's moving at the right speed. The world feels liquid, heavy.

Lorelei goes straight to the drinks table and picks up the punch bowl. Then she locks eyes with me and slowly pours the whole bowl out onto the floor. It splashes onto her feet and her knees, slick and red. The crowd behind me whistles and a couple of people cheer. There are bright lights from people's phones, glittering like stars in the crowd. I wish I could just make everyone disappear right now.

Out of the corner of my eye I see Mrs. Singh approaching me, her blue dress vivid under the lights.

I hold up my free hand to stop her.

"Whatever," Lorelei says, shouting over the music. "I don't want to hear your stupid excuses. I just want you to leave me the fuck alone. Go find someone else to secretly be in love with. Lesbo." For a second I think I see a look of regret on Lorelei's face, but then it vanishes and she scowls.

My heart shifts into my throat and the boulder flips, wild and out of control.

She knows.

Then she takes off out of the gym and I see Mr. Gomez move to go after her, and Mrs. Singh comes to intercept me.

"Julie, are you okay?" Mrs. Singh asks, holding out her hands like there's something she can fix just by touching it.

My face is flushed and my whole body is quaking.

I am not okay, obviously.

I'm still holding Henry's hand and I squeeze it tight. "I just need to talk to her. I think I can fix it," I say. I'm trying to convince myself that's true, but is it? She's known I love her all this time and she never said anything.

Was she just using me?

Is there any part of this friendship that's worth salvaging?

I don't know, but I feel like I need to at least try to find out. There was a second where she looked like she regretted saying all that stuff.

Maybe that means something.

I drop Henry's hand as Mrs. Singh says, "Okay,

if you're sure. I need to find someone to clean up this mess."

"I'll be back," I tell Henry.

He nods. "I'll be here."

I slip out of the hot gym and it's a relief as a whoosh of cold air hits my face. The hallways are super dark and creepy, so I use the wall as a guide and move along as quickly as possible in my wobbly high heels. Lorelei's mad right now, but if I can find her and we can talk, I'm sure I can make her understand.

I did it for her.

So she wouldn't get in trouble.

So all of us wouldn't get in trouble.

She has to know that.

And the whole being in love with her thing—well, that's over now anyway. I've known it for a while now, but I guess I needed tonight to confirm it. This is just about our friendship now—if there's anything left of that.

I check the washroom and front steps, but Lorelei isn't there. If Mr. Gomez caught up with her, they could be in his classroom. That's really the only other option, unless she went home.

As I stumble along away from the gym, the halls get quieter and quieter. And when I finally reach Mr. Gomez's classroom, the door is closed and the lights are off inside. I stand in front of the door in a small puddle of streetlight that's coming from a window just down the hall. The light is the yellow of Lorelei's sheets and walls and carpets, but instead of making me happy it just makes me feel sad and anxious.

I don't regret dumping the booze, but I should have told her. I should have told her that I was in love with her too.

Is it really a real friendship if one friend is secretly in love with the other?

One thing is clear: I've been keeping too many secrets.

Just when I'm about to turn and leave, I hear something from inside the classroom. It sounds like the squeak of a chair on the linoleum floor.

I lean forward to peer through the small square window on the door.

As I press my face against the glass with my hands up to shield out the light, it takes a second for my eyes to adjust.

The silhouettes are dark against the backdrop of the dimly lit classroom windows. It looks like the shadow plays we had to put on in grade three using an incandescent bulb and cardboard cut-outs of people. But Lorelei and Mr. Gomez aren't shadow play: they're all flesh. Lorelei is back up on the desk, only this time she's entwined with Mr. Gomez, his big adult hands on her shoulders, his beak pressed against her face. Her lips on his.

And it all becomes horribly clear.

What I saw that day in the classroom wasn't innocent at all.

And the text when we were getting ready: *Can't wait to see you tonight. <3*

How could Mr. Gomez do this to her? Is Mr. Gomez *actually* in love with her, or did he promise her good grades in exchange for something? Or is she in love with him? The thought makes me sick. It's one thing to joke around that Mr. Gomez is in love with me, or even Lorelei, for that matter; it's another thing entirely for it to actually be true. He's a teacher, an adult. We're just kids. Whether she thinks it's love or not, he shouldn't be taking advantage of her like this. I feel a shiver of disgust crawl down my arms and into my fingertips. This is what keeping secrets gets you: ruined friendships and terrible trysts.

And dead mothers who aren't getting better.

It hits me hard, right in the chest.

I haven't been the hero at all.

I've been keeping this secret about my mom all along, and for what? Because I felt good about being her confidante? Because I thought I could somehow hold the family together all by myself?

Maybe I do need to grow up after all.

"Julie?" It's Mrs. Singh, of course, my shadow in her beautiful blue dress.

I turn around quickly, my heart beating hard in my throat.

"What are you doing?" Mrs. Singh asks. She's holding a mop and she gestures to it, smiling. "I couldn't find the janitor."

"I was just looking for Lorelei," I say.

Now is the time. Be the vault, keep the secret, or let it all go? Mrs. Singh is looking at me, a slight frown on her lips.

"Why would she be in the classroom?" she asks.

I could say she's not.

That there's no one in there.

I could lead her back to the gym so Lorelei and Mr. Gomez could be alone together forever. But that wouldn't be right. And I need to do the right thing. I can't let Mr. Gomez get away with this.

"There's something you need to see," I say.

I turn the handle on the door, open it and flick on the lights.

Now Mrs. Singh is beside me, pulling the door wider and peering into the brightly lit classroom. And she gasps in the way people gasp only when they catch someone doing something they absolutely and unequivocally shouldn't be doing.

As Mrs. Singh pushes past me into the room, Lorelei and Mr. Gomez both turn, their eyes big round Os.

Lorelei's gaze flits from Mrs. Singh to me, then back to Mrs. Singh. I know she knows I was the one who told, but it doesn't matter now because it's over. She probably thinks she'll get in trouble, but this isn't her fault. She's the victim here. And I'm glad Mr. Gomez is caught in the act. It's not right what he's doing, and he needs to know it.

Lorelei narrows her eyes and looks at me with such hatred that it nearly knocks me to the floor.

"I'm sorry," I say. "I had to."

But she doesn't respond. She just looks away with a finality that says it's all over. Our friendship—if you can even call it that. I was holding onto it for so long because it was familiar, because I wanted to believe in it, but now I don't even recognize it anymore. I don't recognize her. Maybe I never did. I just tried to convince myself that we had a best-friendship. That we had something real.

But now it's all done, and I just turn and quietly walk away. I walk down the dark, silent halls and re-enter the gym like everything's normal, but I don't feel like dancing anymore.

This is Lorelei's dance, not mine.

And there's one more secret left to tell.

I circle the dance floor to find Henry.

"How did it go?" he asks.

"Will you come with me?" I say. "There's something I need to do."

He nods and follows me out into the fresh evening air.

Henry and I walk to my house in silence, holding hands. I'm happy that he doesn't ask me any questions, that he seems to know exactly what I need right now.

When we arrive I see my parents through the window. They're on the couch in the living room, watching TV. I take a deep breath and push open the front door, my hand still clasped tight with Henry's, like they're stuck that way and we'll never be able to pry them apart.

"You're home early," Dad says, getting up when we walk into the hall. Mom doesn't say anything; she just keeps staring straight ahead at the TV, which is playing some kind of car commercial.

I smile at him nervously and Dad looks over at Henry, who just shrugs and looks at me.

"I need to show you something, Dad," I say. I'm so anxious my voice is coming out like a tiny flutter.

He frowns and narrows his eyes. "Are you okay?"

"Just bring Mom, okay?"

JC is asleep in his basket beside the couch, and he gives a little sleepy baby sigh and turns over. Dad helps Mom off the couch and I lead the way through the kitchen, into the pantry and down the basement stairs. The single light bulb on the ceiling shines dully, illuminating the coffin with a grey glow.

And now here we are, all four of us staring at the coffin, and Dad says, "Holy shit . . . "

And I just start to talk.

I tell him everything.

Past-tense Mom in the kitchen with a missing heart. Past-tense Mom under his Egyptian cotton sheet on the table in the parlour. Past-tense Mom, silvered by moonlight in the graveyard, buried under a thin layer of earth and Grandpa James's wilting flowers. Past-tense Mom lying in the metal coffin in the Casket Cathedral while Violet pleads for her to rise from the dead. Past-tense Mom as still as a sleeping vampire tucked away in the basement thinking about nothing: breathing no air, eating no food. Mom *was* wonderful. Mom *was* good at her job. Mom *made* good macaroni, once upon a time.

And when I'm done I feel like I weigh nothing at all anymore and if it weren't for Henry standing there, still holding my hand, I might just float, up, up and away.

I look over at Dad but he isn't looking at me. He's staring at Mom like she's a mystery that's just been unravelled.

And she looks over at him and whispers in her flattest, creepiest voice yet:

"I'm dead, Max. I died."

• • •

Mom and Dad have gone upstairs to talk and it's just me and Henry left in the basement. We stand in front of the coffin and stare at it in silence. Then I let go of him and move forward, crack it open and step inside. Because although I feel like I hate it and want it out of my life, I want to see what my mom saw in it. I want to know why she would climb inside day after day. I sit and slide down until I'm lying flat and then I extend my hand to Henry, who climbs in beside me. We fit in perfectly. The two of us, lying on our sides, our faces so close our noses are practically touching. I close my eyes for a second and breathe deep. So this is what it feels like to be in a coffin. Quiet. Peaceful.

I open my eyes. Henry is watching me.

"Hi . . . ," I say.

He laughs.

"I actually think it's possible to be bi," I say. Because I would rather think about my feelings for him than what my mom and dad are talking about upstairs.

"Oh yeah?"

"Yeah. I think you can like boys *and* girls, and I don't think I love Lorelei anymore . . . "

"I'm so sorry about your mom, Julie," he says. As if that's the proper thing to say when a girl is trying to tell you she's in love with you. I push thoughts of Mom's pale face out of my mind.

"It's okay."

"It's not okay."

"But it will be now," I say.

"Julie," Henry says.

"I like the way you say my name. I like the way you do everything, actually."

Then he leans forward and kisses me. It feels completely different from the way I felt when Lorelei kissed me, but not different in a bad way—just different different. I feel the shape of his lips, the curl of his smile. A warm wave travels through me slowly, all the way from my chest to my toes. The boulder in my stomach dissolves, leaving a soft, squishy feeling of happiness in its place. We press ourselves against each other so we're not touching the walls of the coffin; we're just touching the bottom and all of each other. He steals my breath and I steal his and I try to imagine what it would be like to not need breath at all, to just be floating in nothingness and darkness like my mom probably was when she was lying in here. Then I break away from him and reach up to the lid. I close it over our heads so there's just a crack of light left. Just me and Henry and a crack of light, in our metal lifeboat, bobbing on a stormy sea.

15.

When I was fifteen my mom died. Then she came back to life. There are so many things I should have told her. So many things I can tell her now. A eulogy for the living is so much better than one for the dead.

Two whole weeks later and I'm at Mom's bedside at the Centre for Addiction and Mental Health. She looks more colourful, because they're forcing her to eat and drink normally and take medication—all the important stuff you have to do to live. She got diagnosed with something called Cotard's delusion, or Walking Corpse Syndrome. It's often related to schizophrenia and depression and it's really, really rare, so they had to call in like a million different specialists, but whatever they're doing seems to be helping a little because she's more mom-like than she's been in a long time. They say it will take a long time for her to get better, if she can fully recover at all. It's likely the condition will always be with her in some way, but that doesn't mean it has to be her whole life. And at least for now there is some spark of Mom-life in her.

Dad has gone home for a shower so it's just me and Mom and the nurse who is cleaning up Mom's dinner tray.

"You cut your hair," Mom says. She reaches up with her slender but no longer completely skeletal hand and touches my newly shorn locks.

"Yup," I reply, my heart squeezing a little with happiness that she noticed.

The nurse is humming Beethoven's Fifth, and it makes me think that everything's connected to everything else by these thin strands of fate and chance. It's a theory I've been working on lately, but haven't perfected. It makes me think about Lorelei, probably on her way to boarding school right now. After Mr. Gomez was charged, she apologized for everything, but something was lost between us after the dance, something that I can't ever see us getting back.

"You're almost in grade ten." Mom looks wistful for a second, then smiles a little. Probably because she just remembered that high school wasn't all that great.

"Yup," I say again.

"I'm sorry, honey," she says quietly, her eyes looking beyond me to a point above my head.

"For what?" I ask, standing up a little straighter to try to catch her gaze.

"For asking you to keep my secret. I don't know what I was thinking."

I shake my head. "You're sick, Mom. You don't have to be sorry." But the truth is I'm glad she said it. I was worried about telling Dad everything because I didn't want to get in trouble, and I really, truly thought I could handle it by myself. But I see now that none of that was true—that I did the right thing by telling the truth, by reaching out to Dad and getting her proper help.

"But I *am* sorry," she whispers. "Dad and I were already in a bad place. JC put a strain on our relationship. There were tough choices to be made about who would take care of him, and it left us struggling. Then this . . . " She looks down at her hands and I remember all those times at the dining-room table, and the memories make me ache with sadness. I try to shift my focus to something more positive. I think about Henry, the way his smile makes me feel, warm and safe. The way he told me that night in the coffin that he had liked me for a long time, when he was with Lorelei even, and he couldn't believe how happy he was that he got to be with me. He's in the middle of his soccer game right now; I'm going to watch him play when I'm done here.

"It's okay," I whisper back. "We'll get through this together." And for the first time in a long time, I'm confident that it is really, actually okay.

So here's the nurse finishing up with the tray and walking out the door, leaving us really and truly alone. And here's my mom smiling in the sunshine that's streaming through the window. Her eyes are closed and I see little blue veins running through her eyelids, pumping blood toward her heart, which is beating a steady rhythm. *Thump thump. Thump thump.* And now I slip off my shoes and climb into bed with her, like she used to do when I was younger and got the flu. And I wrap my arms around her and look right into her eyes, right into the depths of her soul, and I say really quietly, "I can feel your heartbeat."

And she replies, "Me too."

ACKNOWLEDGEMENTS

This book has been many years in the making and has gone through so many changes to make it what it is today, and I honestly have so many fabulous people to thank for that.

First of all, a huge thank you to my agent, Carrie Plitt of Felicity Bryan Associates. I don't know what I would have done without your patient guidance and amazing suggestions. I want to send a huge thank you to all the judges of the 2015 Word of Mouth contest and the lovely folks at Conville & Walsh for choosing *Past Tense* as runner-up in the contest and believing enough in my book to offer me representation. I also want to thank Zoe Sandler of ICM Partners for falling in love with Julie and working hard on her behalf in the United States.

Next I would like to thank my awesome editor

Acknowledgements

at HarperCollins, Suzanne Sutherland. I was so honoured and thrilled to have been able to work with you, and your edits really made the story shine. Thank you for all your time and effort; it is so appreciated. A huge thank you as well to the entire team at HarperCollins, including Stephanie Nuñez and Linda Pruessen, for believing in my book, working with me and giving *Past Tense* a chance to get out into the world.

I would like to send a big thank you out to my writing groups that have heard at least one of the incarnations of this book and offered valuable feedback to my opening chapters. To the Ashdale Writers Group: you have been there for me since the beginning of this journey, and I can't thank you enough for your support over the years. To the Eggs—Deb, Jack and Bill (RIP): you three are such an inspiration. To the Ink Group: although our time together was short, it was so valuable.

To Alice, an early reader and friend: thank you so much for your feedback and your unending support.

To my mom, Heather: thank you for loving the heck out of me, no matter how much trouble I was, and for making me believe I could do anything I set my mind to. And my dad, Jim: thanks for passing on your love of writing (and the writing gene) and encouraging me to always be my own dog. I love you both so much.

Acknowledgements

To Dan and Mel and Rowan and Ryder: you all rock and I'm so glad you're back in my life. And to the Loughead & Orsini clan: thanks for the support and for being an awesome family-in-law.

Thank you to the wonderful Sharlena, for inspiring me with your creativity and encouraging me to keep writing even when the road is rough.

And finally to Ben, my amazing hero of a husband who has read so many versions of this story that he should win some sort of award. I really couldn't have done any of this without you, and I love you more than words could ever even begin to express.